AN UNE

LOVE

Ravina walked across to the barred nursery window and stared out across the gardens and orchards to where she could just see the edge of the cliff that protected the house from the sea.

"Indeed, Sir Richard, I think the Manor would make a lovely home, but even with servants, you might find it a little large living here on your own."

He placed his hand on the rocking horse and gave it a gentle push, watching the curved runners making little marks on the dusty floor.

"I am hoping that I will not be alone. There is a lady whom I would like to ask to be my wife and then – "

"Ouch!" Ravina winced. She had clutched the iron bars at the window so hard that a little sliver of metal had sliced into her finger.

Sir Richard intended to marry! This house was being prepared for his wife.

She felt a surge of anger and despair. He had no right to bring her here, to ask her opinion of its suitability. That was the prerogative of the lady to whom he would be offering his hand and his heart.

She had no idea why she should feel so upset. After all, this man was a stranger, he meant nothing to her!

Nothing at all.

THE BARBARA CARTLAND PINK COLLECTION

Titles in this series

AN UNEXPECTED LOVE

BARBARA CARTLAND

Barbaracartland.com Ltd

Copyright © 2007 by Cartland Promotions

First published on the internet in June
2007 by Barbaracartland.com

ISBN 978-1-905155-42-2

Printed and bound in Great Britain by CLE Print Ltd,
St Ives, Cambridgeshire

THE BARBARA CARTLAND PINK COLLECTION

Barbara Cartland was the most prolific bestselling author in the history of the world. She was frequently in the Guinness Book of Records for writing more books in a year than any other living author. In fact her most amazing literary feat was when her publishers asked for more Barbara Cartland romances, she doubled her output from 10 books a year to over 20 books a year, when she was 77.

She went on writing continuously at this rate for 20 years and wrote her last book at the age of 97, thus completing 400 books between the ages of 77 and 97.

Her publishers finally could not keep up with this phenomenal output, so at her death she left 160 unpublished manuscripts, something again that no other author has ever achieved.

Now the exciting news is that these 160 original unpublished Barbara Cartland books are already being published and by Barbaracartland.com exclusively on the internet, as the international web is the best possible way of reaching so many Barbara Cartland readers around the world.

The 160 books are published monthly and will be numbered in sequence.

The series is called the Pink Collection as a tribute to Barbara Cartland whose favourite colour was pink and it became very much her trademark over the years.

The Barbara Cartland Pink Collection is published only on the internet. Log on to www.barbaracartland.com to find out how you can purchase the books monthly as they are published, and take out a subscription that will ensure that all subsequent editions are delivered to you by mail order to your home.

NEW

Barbaracartland.com is proud to announce the publication of ten new Audio Books for the first time as CDs. They are favourite Barbara Cartland stories read by well-known actors and actresses and each story extends to 4 or 5 CDs. The Audio Books are as follows :

The Patient Bridegroom	The Passion and the Flower
A Challenge of Hearts	Little White Doves of Love
A Train to Love	The Prince and the Pekinese
The Unbroken Dream	A King in Love
The Cruel Count	A Sign of Love

More Audio Books will be published in the future and the above titles can be purchased by logging on to the website www.barbaracartland.com or please write to the address below.

If you do not have access to a computer, you can write for information about the Barbara Cartland Pink Collection and the Barbara Cartland Audio Books to the following address :

Barbara Cartland.com Ltd.
Camfield Place,
Hatfield,
Hertfordshire AL9 6JE
United Kingdom.
Telephone: +44 (0)1707 642629
Fax: +44 (0)1707 663041

THE LATE DAME BARBARA CARTLAND

Barbara Cartland who sadly died in May 2000 at the age of nearly 99 was the world's most famous romantic novelist who wrote 723 books in her lifetime with worldwide sales of over 1 billion copies and her books were translated into 36 different languages.

As well as romantic novels, she wrote historical biographies, 6 autobiographies, theatrical plays, books of advice on life, love, vitamins and cookery. She also found time to be a political speaker and television and radio personality.

She wrote her first book at the age of 21 and this was called *Jigsaw*. It became an immediate bestseller and sold 100,000 copies in hardback and was translated into 6 different languages. She wrote continuously throughout her life, writing bestsellers for an astonishing 76 years. Her books have always been immensely popular in the United States, where in 1976 her current books were at numbers 1 & 2 in the B. Dalton bestsellers list, a feat never achieved before or since by any author.

Barbara Cartland became a legend in her own lifetime and will be best remembered for her wonderful romantic novels, so loved by her millions of readers throughout the world.

Her books will always be treasured for their moral message, her pure and innocent heroines, her good looking and dashing heroes and above all her belief that the power of love is more important than anything else in everyone's life.

"Mankind can reach the stars, but only through pure love."

Barbara Cartland

CHAPTER ONE
1896

The glittering crystal chandeliers sparkled and gleamed casting their golden light on the waltzing couples below.

High up in the gallery above the ballroom, resplendent in yellow with gold braid across their chests, the musicians, faces red and shining with heat, were playing the latest dance tunes with verve and gusto.

To an onlooker, the highly polished floor of the ballroom of Lyall House in the most fashionable part of London was a kaleidoscope of colour, the white tie and tails of the gentlemen a perfect foil for the glorious dresses of their partners.

And no one looked more glorious than Lady Ravina Ashley as she whirled round the floor in the arms of the millionaire industrialist, Mr. Robert Dunster.

Her honey-coloured hair was styled in the latest fashion, held fast in its elaborate twist by a diamond and sapphire clip.

And although her cream lace dress was not cut as daringly low as those of some of the ladies present, it still showed off her beautiful figure to its full advantage.

The pearl necklet and matching earbobs might not

glitter as much as the diamonds some of the older ladies wore, but they shone with a warm glow against her translucent skin.

Her partner was a good dancer for such a heavily built man, but the energetic exercise was obviously not to his liking.

His shirt collar looked wet where it dug into a red fleshy neck and Ravina was only too aware that the hands holding her were damp and sticky.

She wished he had thought to wear white gloves as so many other gentlemen did.

She cast a look from under her thick dark lashes at Robert Dunster's red face, listening to his rasping breathing as they circled the room once more and made a swift decision.

She stumbled a little on the next spin and put a hand to her forehead.

"Goodness, the heat is making me feel faint, Mr. Dunster. I am so sorry, but do you think we could sit down for a while?"

The industrialist looked concerned and promptly guided her through the circling couples to the side of the room and off the dance floor.

"It is indeed extremely close in here, Lady Ravina. Far too many couples, I am afraid. I did tell Lord Lyall that he had invited an excess of people, but I am afraid, as usual, my comments fell on deaf ears."

Ravina smiled, hardly listening to his words. She did not mind dancing with him, but his self-importance was extremely irritating.

She had met him twice before and did not have a good opinion of the man.

Admittedly he was extremely polite and correct, but he

always seemed to know better than everyone else, always had an opinion that could not be shaken, even if he was proved wrong.

"Perhaps I might fetch you an ice or a cooling glass of lemonade?" he was saying as she flicked open the ivory fan that hung from her wrist.

"What? Oh, no thank you, Mr. Dunster. It is getting quite late, I see. I must be thinking of going home soon. I came with the Ross family and I am sure they will not be staying much longer. Lady Ross does not like to be out too late."

He pushed wide the French windows that opened out onto the paved terrace that ran the length of the ballroom.

Coloured lanterns had been hung in the trees and bushes in the garden and the moon sailed serenely through the midnight sky.

Several couples were sitting on little metal chairs, talking, laughing and enjoying the soft evening breeze that was rustling the trees in Berkley Square.

"I saw Lord Ross going into the billiard room only ten minutes ago. I believe he is very involved in a competition between some of the older gentlemen. I think you will have plenty of time to sit in the garden and cool down before your journey home, Lady Ravina."

Ravina hesitated and then walked out into the night air. She had to admit it was refreshing to feel the coolness on her hot cheeks.

"This tradition of always being accompanied to a ball can be very tiresome," she said as they walked slowly along a mossy path that meandered towards steps into the rose garden.

"But a young lady such as yourself cannot travel around London on her own."

Ravina tossed her head, her sapphire blue eyes

flashing. This was exactly the sort of remark that made her irritable.

"Indeed, Mr. Dunster, I am quite capable of attending a ball on my own. I could have organised my transport this evening very easily, and then I would not be dependent on Lord Ross's billiard game deciding the time of my departure."

They reached the rose garden where huge swathes of sweet smelling flowers hung from columns and arches.

The moon was hiding behind a cloud now, but even in the dim light, the reds and pinks and yellows of the velvety petals gleamed in glorious abundance.

Ravina took a deep breath, glorying in the marvellous scents that filled the air.

She wandered across to a raised lily pond, admiring the splashing of the fountain and peering into the water to catch a glimpse of one of Lord Lyall's famous koi carp.

Robert Dunster plucked a crimson bud from a bush and twirled it between his fingers.

"You have very modern views on life, Lady Ravina," he commented tersely.

"We will soon be nearing a new century," Ravina replied, returning to his side. "Who knows what lies ahead of us in our amazing world. I do not wish to be held back from experiencing life just because I am a woman."

The heavily built businessman frowned and then gave a muffled curse as he caught his finger on a thorn.

"Your parents, Lord and Lady Ashley, are away a great deal, I believe."

Ravina sighed, gazing up at the stars in the sky.

"Yes, Papa is in the Foreign Office, as you know, and he and Mama have to travel abroad regularly."

"Are they absent now?"

Ravina glanced at him curiously. There had been a strangely tense note in his voice.

"No, they are at home, sir."

She was pleased to be able to say that. She adored her parents and it was a great sadness to her that she was alone such a great deal.

When they were all together, either in London or at their Dorset estate, they were such a happy and contented family. Her parents' frequent absences abroad always made her unhappy.

But she had too resilient a nature to be miserable for long. Her high spirits bubbled up now and she swung round to Robert Dunster.

Then she gasped! For a second, she thought he was trying to put his arms round her!

He was standing extremely close and she could see the little red veins on his cheeks and a pulse beating frantically in his temple.

Even as she tried to step backwards, she realised there was a stone bench directly behind her stopping her from moving.

His hands reached out and grasped her shoulders.

"Careful, Lady Ravina, you might fall and hurt yourself."

Ravina eased herself away and sat down on the bench. For some reason she was shaking. How silly. The heat must have made her dizzy. She was not the sort of girl who fainted at every awkward moment.

"I think I could drink that lemonade now, if you would be so kind."

He gave a little bow, his jacket straining across his broad shoulders.

"Of course. My pleasure. I will be back as soon as I can."

He strode away and Ravina struggled to regain her composure, but she was still feeling strangely unnerved when a footfall on the path made her spin around.

But it was not Mr. Dunster returning, rather a young man she had known since she was a child. It was Viscount Giles de Lacey, heir to the Marquis of Harmon.

Tall and thin with prominent blue eyes and a thatch of brown hair that refused to lie flat, the young man seemed all arms and legs.

His evening clothes always looked as if they belonged to someone else. The sleeves appeared too short for his arms and he was showing far too much cuff to be fashionable.

Ravina sighed. She was quite sure that she knew what was going to happen next and she really was not in the mood for Giles tonight.

He was her exact age, born on the same day, and their parents were great friends. The two babies had lain next to each other in their cradles and Giles had been her faithful admirer since they were children, playing musical chairs at their joint birthday parties.

Once they had both celebrated their eighteenth birthdays, never a party, ball, race meeting or pheasant shoot had passed without him proposing marriage to her.

"Ravina, how lovely you look tonight. Like a young Goddess."

"Oh, Giles, don't be silly. Do go away."

The young man sat down on the bench next to her, smiling happily like a large puppy dog.

"I saw you dancing with Robert Dunster. I say, Rav, you know you should be damned careful of that gentleman. He hasn't got a particularly good reputation, you know."

Ravina snapped open her little ivory fan again and tried to wave some cooler air across her face. Giles was so annoying.

6

"Anyway, that's not what I came to say. Let's forget Dunster. There! I have already. Ravina, listen to me."

He reached over and took her hands in his, stilling the fan in mid beat, crushing her rings against her fingers.

"You know how I feel about you. I adore and worship you, Ravina. And obviously the old money's no object and when Pater goes, I will have the title and the castle and the land. We could have such a good life together and, oh, Ravina, I do love you so much. *Please*, please marry me."

Ravina raised her eyebrows in exasperation. Usually she could laugh at Giles and tease him about his devotion.

She was well versed in all the platitudes she had learnt from her mother when confronted by a proposal of marriage you did not solicit or welcome.

Ravina could usually make Giles admit that proposing to her had become a habit with him, that one day he would meet a girl who would make a perfect Marchioness, but it would *not* be Ravina.

She would agree to be Godmother to his first child and he would agree to be Godfather to hers. They always parted the best of friends.

But tonight was different. In some odd way, Mr. Dunster had left her feeling unsettled and irritable and the young man's words annoyed her.

"Giles," she snapped crossly. "Don't be so silly. You know perfectly well I am never going to marry you. Why do you persist in asking me? I do wish you would stop. It is so very wearying."

"But Ravina, sweetheart – "

"Please do not call me that stupid name. It makes you sound ridiculous. You know I don't like you in that way. I will *never* like you in that way. Who would?"

She bit her lip as her childhood friend flinched as if

7

she had pinched him. The colour drained from his face and he scowled.

Ravina was overcome with shame.

Giles was a dear boy and did not deserve this treatment. She knew her mother would be appalled at her behaviour if she ever found out.

"Giles, I am sorry – " she began, but the gangling youth had stood up, surprisingly dignified for all his ungainliness.

"I quite accept that I am not good enough for you, Ravina," he said stiffly. "And I can only apologise for intruding and spoiling the ball for you. I will take my leave and wish you a pleasant evening."

With a brief nod he turned and walked away, stumbling slightly as he mounted the steps out of the rose garden.

Ravina jumped to her feet about to run after him when a sudden sound made her stop and spin round.

A stranger appeared from behind a tall trellis, heavy with huge white roses that scattered their petals like snow on the ground at his feet.

He was slim and very dark, immaculate in evening dress. His deep brown eyes were serious in a tanned face that to Ravina looked disapproving.

"Sir?" she said bravely. "A gentleman does not eavesdrop on a private conversation."

The stranger bowed.

"Madam, a young lady should not be so hard-hearted when listening to a proposal of marriage."

Ravina felt hot colour rush up into her cheeks.

She knew the stranger was right to condemn her behaviour, but he could not be aware of the relationship between her and Giles, so he was judging her on false assumptions.

"So you believe I should have simpered and smiled and told Giles de Lacey that he did me an incredible honour in thinking I was suitable to be his future wife?"

The dark haired man took another step forward and at that moment the moon sailed out from behind a cloud and bathed the rose garden in silver light. It struck a beam from the diamond clip in Ravina's hair, making it glitter like ice.

From the house, the band struck up a new tune, a polka this time.

Ravina glanced round, wondering crossly where Robert Dunster was with her lemonade. His arrival would at least mean this man could not continue to lecture her.

"I believe you could have let the young Viscount down more gently," the tall stranger said. "He was offering you his heart and his life. Surely *not* an inconsiderable gift."

Angrily, Ravina snapped her fan open. She knew he was right, but there was something about this man that brought her stubborn streak to the fore.

"Oh, I see, sir. Well, I hope that if you ever propose marriage, your future wife will be as thrilled by the offer of your name as you obviously think she should be."

There was a moment's silence and as Ravina lifted her chin and stared into his dark unfathomable eyes, she thought she saw a flash of pain cross his face.

But then it was gone and, to her astonishment, he was reaching out and with one finger, touched the cream lace frill where it cascaded down over her upper arm.

"You seem to have a blood stain on your dress, madam. I would suggest you try to remove it as soon as possible. And take care, Lady Ravina. There are thorns that bite in every relationship."

And with a severe bow, he turned and vanished into

the dark gardens.

Ravina glanced down at the frill and bit her lip. The odious man was right. A small blood stain marked the lace.

She realised straight away that it must be from Mr. Dunster's finger. The thorn on the rose he had picked must have bitten deep and when he grasped her arm to stop her falling, he had marked her dress.

She shuddered. She hated the sight of blood, especially on her clothes.

Picking up her full cream lace skirt, Ravina moved swiftly away from the rose garden. She did not want to stay and speak to Robert Dunster again.

The stranger had annoyed her so much.

But as she headed for the house, determined to find her friends and insist that they go home, she did wonder how he had known her name, because she knew she had never met him before. He was not the type of man you would easily forget.

Ravina was not in a good mood when she finally arrived at Ashley House, the London home in Knightsbridge belonging to her father, the Earl of Ashley.

Steven, the night-footman on duty, opened the front door as she stepped out of the Ross's coach, said her thank yous and goodnights and ran swiftly up the steps.

"My Lady," he murmured as she flounced into the house, pulling off her long white gloves and throwing them carelessly on the beautiful inlaid hall table.

"Hello, Steven. Heavens, I am tired. I think I have danced too much. Are my parents still downstairs?"

"No, my Lady. They have retired for the evening. But Nanny Johnson is waiting for you in her room, I believe. She asked me to tell you that she would not be retiring until she knew you were home."

"Goodness, why on earth does she do this?" Ravina said crossly. "She should have been in bed hours ago. Steven, can you arrange for me to have a cup of tea and some biscuits in my room, please? I am starving."

The footman grinned as she dropped her evening cloak on the floor and headed for the stairs.

He picked up the heavy ruby silk garment with a sigh. Lady Ravina had ruled this house ever since she was born, but the staff knew that beneath her sometimes careless attitude lay a kind and affectionate person.

He wondered as he headed back below stairs if she had received any more proposals that evening. She had been portrayed in the newspapers as being one of the prettiest *debutantes* London had ever seen.

Bets were being laid between the staff as to who exactly would win her hand.

Unaware that her private life was the subject of such discussion between the servants, Ravina ran up the main staircase.

She passed her own bedroom and up another smaller flight to the suite of rooms that had once been the day nursery, the night nursery and the bedroom that was now the permanent home of Nanny Johnson.

Ravina knocked on the door and, without waiting for a reply, opened it and hurried inside.

"Ah, there you are. Back at last, miss."

Nanny Johnson was old. How old Ravina did not know. She had been her nanny, her father's before that and had even been a nursemaid to Ravina's grandfather when he was a baby!

Small and wrinkled as an old apple, she always wore black with a white lace cap and, Ravina thought, mischievously, looked exactly like pictures of Queen Victoria, who was also very old.

Ravina realised she must never, never tell her because to Nanny the Royal family were the most important people in the world and being told she resembled the dear Queen would, in her eyes, be close to treason.

"Really, Nanny, you do not have to stay up every time I go out at night," she said, trying to quell the irritation in her voice.

She looked up from the crochet work in her gnarled hands.

"I do not care to hear that tone from you, Lady Ravina. It is unpleasant. And take that frown off your face or else the wind will change and you will be left with it forever."

Ravina sank to the floor next to the old lady's rocking chair and leant against her rough black skirt.

She felt her bad mood slipping away. Nanny could always soothe her when she was troubled.

Ravina could remember a time she had been plagued by nightmares when she was a small child – caused by the terrifying stories her nursemaid had told her.

Her parents had been abroad and Nanny Johnson had been the only person who could calm her fears and discover why she was so upset.

Nanny's fire had been lit earlier in the evening and the embers left in the grate sparked and flared.

"Nanny, Giles de Lacey proposed to me *again* tonight."

Nanny clicked her tongue in annoyance, but her hand reached down to stroke the blonde curls at her knee.

"And you said no, I hope."

"Of course. But why does he keep doing it? I like Giles, but – "

"He is more a brother to you," Nanny said wisely. "And you have grown up enough to see it, but young Lord de Lacey has not. He will one day though, don't you fret, my dear. Then he will set his eyes on some young girl, probably Lord Lyall's youngest – the red-headed one and marry her."

"Well, I wish he would hurry up and do so," Ravina yawned. "Oh, and I danced with Mr. Robert Dunster – twice."

Nanny's fingers stilled on the white cotton she was twisting into intricate shapes.

"You are surely not attracted to him?"

Ravina gazed into the dying embers of the fire and absentmindedly rubbed the place on her dress where his blood had stained it.

"No, certainly not. Undoubtedly he is a clever man, rich and powerful, but he has not shown any interest in me in that way."

"And if he did?"

Ravina laughed softly then shuddered as she recalled the industrialist's hot hands and the collar of his shirt digging into that pink fleshy neck.

"Oh, no, Nanny. I could never marry him. I know lots of girls in Society marry for a name or to join two great families together, but I want to fall in love with the man I marry.

"I want to experience all the passion and drama and desire that I have read about in books such as *Jane Eyre* and *Wuthering Heights*."

"Tosh and nonsense," Nanny Johnson said with a little smile. "Off to bed with you now or you will become so ugly from lack of sleep that no one will ever want to marry you and you will end up an old maid."

*

But later that night, as Ravina lay in bed, staring out of her window at the starry sky, she knew that her words to

Nanny Johnson had been the truth.

It would be stupid for her not to recognise the fact that as the only child of the Earl of Ashley, she would be a prize catch for lots of men.

Her father was a powerful man in politics. Exactly what he did at the Foreign Office, Ravina was not sure, but she did know that people came from all over the world to their house to seek his advice and help.

Anyone who married his daughter would have an exceptional chance of preferment.

Ravina had learned from the age of sixteen that proposals of marriage were never hard to come by. But she had never been tempted to say yes.

She had always asked herself the same question,

'Would I be happy with him? Would I be content to belong to no one but him? To do what *he* wants rather than what *I* want and to concentrate on his way of life, instead of the freedom I have at the moment to do exactly what excites me and not ask any man if that is what he wants to do too.'

With her eyes closed and a soft pillow beneath her head, she told herself that life was so exciting and very interesting as it was.

For the moment at any rate she had no wish for anything different.

'Perhaps one day I will find it impossible not to be so much in love that when a man asks me to marry him I can only say '*yes, yes, yes*' and throw myself into his arms,' she told herself.

She smiled in the dark.

'That is just what I want,' she said almost aloud, 'and perhaps one day I will be very happy, wildly and gloriously happy, because I will want nothing but the man I love and the man who loves me.'

This was the promise she had made herself, that she would never marry except when she felt a deep devoted love for a good man. A love that was returned in every way.

Which, she thought as she turned over at last on her cool snowy pillows to fall asleep, was probably much more than the bride of that odious dark-eyed stranger in the rose garden would ever know!

CHAPTER TWO

Ravina was very late for breakfast the next morning. She sped down the shining wooden staircase into the hall of Ashley House, the skirts of her pink silk morning dress rustling as she hurried.

Her parents were already seated at the table in the breakfast room, her father busy reading *The Times* and her mother opening her letters.

Ravina leant over and kissed her father on the forehead, smiling at the usual gruff "good morning, child, you are late."

Lord Ashley was a tall, thin, distinguished man in his late forties. Like his father and his grandfather before him, he held a high position in the Foreign Office.

Ravina had grown up with political discussions with high-ranking foreign officials taking place around her.

She had often escaped from her nanny and governesses to hide under her father's big desk in the library.

She had played happily with her dolls and toys whilst talk of trouble in the Balkans, revolutions and wars were discussed over her head.

As she grew older and was included officially at dinners and luncheons, she had met several foreign heads of state and Prime Ministers.

She had learnt how vitally important her father's work

was for European peace. He was adept at defusing potentially explosive situations and Ravina recognised that only his skill at diplomacy had prevented a number of nasty situations from deteriorating into war.

Her geography lessons had always been easy for her because her parents had travelled all over Europe and she had often accompanied them, much to Nanny Johnson's annoyance.

Nanny had very firm views about the place a young lady should take in Society.

Lady Ashley was small and slender and Ravina was already taller than her. But she had the same honey-gold hair as her daughter and her delicate appearance was at odds with her ability to cope with all the demands made of her as the wife of a senior diplomat.

This morning she was dressed in deepest lilac, her wide sleeves narrowing to tight cuffs that emphasised the whiteness of her elegant hands and the gleaming diamonds and amethysts that adorned them.

She shook her head in mock resignation as Ravina kissed her cheek and slid into her chair, ignoring her father's scowl.

Being late for a meal was something Lord Ashley hated. He said it was impolite to the cook to eat the food half cold.

One of the footmen poured Ravina a cup of coffee and she helped herself to bread and honey.

"So, darling, did you enjoy yourself last night at the ball?" her mother asked. "You were very late arriving home."

"Not too late really, Mama. And yes, I had a very nice time. Giles was there, of course. And lots of the usual people."

"And I suppose Giles proposed again," her mother

smiled. Like Ravina, she was sure that the young man was not even slightly in love with her daughter. His heart would not even be dented by her constant refusals.

Ravina frowned, remembering the dark-haired, sarcastic man in the rose garden.

But she was not going to tell her parents about him. Her reaction to Giles had not been correct and she knew that her mother would not be pleased.

'Poor Giles. Perhaps,' Ravina thought, 'I should have said yes and settled down to be a good wife and the mother of several delightful children. Giles enjoys travelling as I do. And when he inherits the castle, he will have a splendid life. Would that have been such a bad life to share? A girl could do far worse.'

Then it was almost as if someone was asking her,

'So why do you always say no, instead of yes?'

And she knew that the answer was that Giles would never touch her heart. And there must be so much more to marriage than pleasant convenience – surely?

She jumped slightly as her father folded away his newspaper and glanced across the table at his daughter with his piercing gaze.

"Did you by any chance meet a Mr. Robert Dunster at the ball last night, Ravina?"

"Mr. Dunster? Why yes, Papa, I did. I danced with him twice and he offered to bring me a cold lemonade in the garden when I was very hot."

"I see. And was he – polite?" Lord Ashley seemed to find his coffee cup extremely interesting.

Ravina felt bewildered by his question.

"Certainly, Papa. Why, do people speak badly of his manners? He certainly gave me no cause to be upset."

She caught her parents exchanging glances and her

18

puzzlement grew. Her father seemed worried, as if he had something on his mind.

"No, no, I am sure his behaviour would be impeccable. Indeed, I have heard nothing that could be held against him, except that he is a hard-headed business man. But he does have a reputation for asking questions to gain information.

"I would have been unhappy if you had been upset and if he had been pestering you in any way – asking where your mother and I were, for example. Why we were not attending the ball. That type of thing."

"Well, he did ask me if you were at home or travelling abroad. But only in a very polite general way. We discussed nothing of importance, Papa. I have met him before, but this is the first time I have danced with him. Do you wish me to avoid him in future?"

"No, certainly not," her father replied.

"Ravina, dear," her mother now broke in, "your father and I have something to tell you. We are going abroad for a few weeks."

Ravina pushed back her chair. This was news indeed.

"Abroad? When? And am I to accompany you, Mama?"

"We leave tomorrow and no, you will not be coming with us this time, darling. It is strictly a business trip and you might well be bored."

Lady Ashley looked fondly at her beautiful daughter.

"But we are concerned about you staying here on your own so we intend to shut up this house for the duration of our absence. We feel you will be far happier in the country at Curbishley Hall."

Ravina nodded, her mind racing.

"Well, I will certainly be sad to miss some of the London parties, but you know I love the countryside and I have been pining for my horses while I have been here in London."

"And Cousin Dulcie will be there as chaperone and company for you. I am sure that Nanny Johnson will travel down to Dorset too, but Dulcie is family after all and much closer to your own age."

Ravina screwed up her nose. She liked Dulcie Allen, but at twenty-eight, the older girl was a confirmed spinster and disapproved of her young cousin acting in any way she felt forward or improper.

Dulcie's father had been a distant cousin of Lord Ashley, but when he died it was discovered that he was heavily in debt.

Dulcie was an only child – her mother had died when she was born and overnight she had lost her father, her home and her genteel way of life.

Lord Ashley had heard of her plight and invited her to come and live at Curbishley Hall. She was to be the housekeeper, look after the house when the family was in London and be a companion to Ravina when she visited Dorset.

Dulcie had been only too happy to accept.

'Oh well,' Ravina thought, 'I can get round Dulcie easily enough. She hates horses, so she will not be accompanying me out riding. I can still have plenty of fun.'

"Are you quite sure you will be happy in the country by yourself?" her mother asked, a worried look marring her lovely face. "We could send you to Ireland to my parents, if you would prefer."

Ravina laughed and spread more honey on her toast.

"I love Ireland but I love Dorset best. I will be quite happy, Mama. I shall ride and visit friends, shop in Rosbourne and I will even try and help Dulcie in the garden – if she will let me. Last time I dug up all her lettuces thinking they were weeds!"

Lady Ashley looked at her daughter and could not help thinking how unbelievably pretty she was. With her dark gold hair, bright blue eyes and creamy pink skin, she was the picture of a young English rose.

At the same time, she knew that in many ways her daughter was different from other girls of the same age.

She sighed and thought,

'She has inherited her father's stubborn nature but, as yet, there is no sign of his diplomatic abilities. I wonder exactly what type of man will be prepared to marry a girl who will not agree with everything he says and will want to go her own way in the world.'

She was not surprised that although Ravina had been 'out' for a year, there had not been any exceptional love interest, which she might have been delighted about for her daughter's sake.

"The whole trouble with Ravina," she had said to her husband, "is that she is too attractive. She is also very intelligent and I think that until she learns to hide that fact, men will be scared of marrying her."

"Rubbish, my dear. If that is the case, then the man who does make her his wife will be very special indeed, which is just as it should be.

"I would not have her wed anyone less than a man who admires and loves her for herself alone and not be influenced by the fact that she is my daughter and heir to our estate."

But now, as Lady Ashley watched her husband and daughter discussing which horses in his stables at Curbishley Hall needed to be exercised and for how long, she knew that she was still worried.

This was not a good time to be leaving Ravina on her own, but there was no choice. That was the problem that duty brought with it. Sometimes you were forced to make sacrifices for the sake of the country that affected your nearest and dearest.

*

The next morning dawned bright and still, a perfect day to start a foreign trip, Ravina thought.

All was hustle and bustle in the house as the trunks and cases, hat boxes and travelling bags were assembled in the hall and carried out to the carriage.

"Please do not stay away too long, dearest Mama," Ravina implored, trying to hug her mother but finding it difficult as her small personage was hidden beneath a large pink hat covered in feathers.

"I will miss you both, but at least I will have lots of new stories to hear when you get back."

Lord Ashley appeared, pulling on his gloves.

"Take great care of yourself, Ravina," he said, his voice serious. "And try not to get into any mischief. Rely on Dulcie's good sense to guide you if you are in any doubt. And if trouble comes calling, show it the door."

Ravina laughed and kissed him affectionately.

"I will do my best, Papa," she promised, "but odd things do happen to me as you very well know. But if they do, I shall rely on you coming to my rescue when you return."

She watched enviously as her mother's maid and her father's valet were driven away in the small carriage and next the larger coach appeared from the mews, her parents climbed in and Ravina stood waving goodbye until it was lost to view.

The slim golden-haired girl stood for a while on the front steps, admiring the sweep of the crescent where Ashley House was situated

22

The neigh of a horse made her look round.

A rider, heavily cloaked, was turning his mount in the road, as if he had changed his mind and no longer wished to ride past the house.

Even from a distance, Ravina could admire the beautiful grey stallion the man was riding.

She wondered which of their neighbours owned such a horse and strained her eyes to see who it was.

But she realised the distance was too far and her eyes must be deceiving her, because she could have sworn that the horseman was, in fact, the dark-eyed stranger who had been so rude to her in the rose garden at the ball.

She half raised her hand to gesture to him, but by then he was trotting away back down the road.

'Perhaps he is a guest at one of the other houses in the Crescent,' she thought and wondered which of her neighbours he could be visiting.

As she walked back across the hall, she said to Gibbs, the butler,

"As you know, I shall be leaving for the country tomorrow morning, Gibbs. Will you please inform George that I intend to drive myself."

She saw him frown, but his training overcame his natural desire to interfere and he merely replied,

"Yes, my Lady."

Ravina was faced with all the decisions that went with packing up a great house and moving herself and the staff to the country.

She had to arrange which servants should travel with her and which remain in London to make sure the rooms were kept well aired and cleaned, ready for her parents when they returned home.

Nanny Johnson would be accompanying Ravina and

so would Gibbs, Mrs. Crandle, the head cook, and several of her staff.

Mrs. Crandle was a marvellous cook, but a real dragon and she knew that there would be tension between her and the cook at Curbishley Hall.

Ravina sighed as she answered a multitude of questions and decided which of her clothes to take and which to leave behind.

She paused briefly in front of her dressing table mirror and tidied her hair. She gazed at her reflection in the mirror.

It was a shame that she would miss so many parties and balls over the next few weeks.

"Oh, well, I am certain someone locally will be giving a ball while I am in Dorset," she said to Charity, her maid, who was busy packing her trunk.

"I can think of lots of friends in Rosbourne who are sure to be in party mood. I think we had better be prepared, so pack both the ivory, pink and blue evening gowns. And do not forget the shoes."

She ran down the stairs, heading for the music room to collect the sheet music she had been playing recently.

Ravina knew she was not as good a pianist as her cousin Dulcie, but she enjoyed accompanying her mother when she sang at evening soirées.

The piano at Curbishley Hall was very fine and it would be a pleasure to play it once more.

"There is a visitor, my Lady," Gibbs announced gravely, crossing the hall as she appeared. "I have asked him to wait in the drawing room."

"Oh, thank you, Gibbs. Who is it?"

"A Sir Michael Moore, my Lady. Asking for his Lordship."

Ravina paused, her hand on the door knob. She had

met Sir Michael briefly a few weeks earlier at a race meeting at Epsom and he had asked her to join a theatre party to see one of Mr. Barrie's new plays.

But she already had an engagement for that evening and so declined.

She wondered what Sir Michael could possibly want with her father and then remembered that he was as interested in horses as Lord Ashley.

When she entered the room, Ravina found him standing in front of the fireplace. He was a pleasant-faced, well built man in his late thirties, wearing a plain but well-cut suit.

He had a 'no nonsense' air about him and Ravina could imagine him giving brisk orders in whatever he undertook in life.

"Good morning, Sir Michael. This is a very early visit."

He held out his hand and stepped forward.

"Good morning, Lady Ravina. I do apologise for disturbing you, but I have called to ask your father for his advice, only to find that he and your mother have just left to go abroad."

"I am sure Papa will be very sorry to have missed the chance of helping you," Ravina replied. "Were you, perhaps, going to ask his advice about your racehorses? I believe you have quite a few and have been most successful."

"Yes, indeed. I have a fine string of thoroughbreds, but my knowledge is not as great as your father's, which is why I came here this morning."

He stopped and then ventured,

"And are you staying in London while your parents are away?"

"No," Ravina replied, walking across the room to sit

on a small leather sofa. "I am leaving soon to go to our country estate in Dorset."

"Ah, good," Sir Michael hesitated, "I was telling your father when we met at our Club last week that my house, which has been in my family for generations, is only about three miles from Curbishley Hall."

She smiled politely and he continued,

"My father was very ill for many years before he died. He and my mother had travelled on business to Australia and he was too ill to return home. So the house was shut up and left.

"I inherited a small racing stable from my aunt and I have lived until now near Newmarket, but when my mother died last year, the Priory became mine."

Ravina looked up, her eyes sparkling.

"Oh, I know now which house is yours. An ancient building you see when you ride beside our woodlands. But surely the Priory is a ruin?"

Sir Michael smiled and shook his head.

"It was, but is no longer. I have been restoring it all year. In fact, another reason for my visit today was to ask your parents if they would like to attend a dinner party I am planning to mark the Priory's glorious resurrection."

"I am sure they will be sorry to miss it."

Sir Michael looked up eagerly.

"As you will be at Curbishley Hall, perhaps you would be my guest?"

Ravina clapped her hands together.

"Oh, thank you, Sir Michael, I would indeed love to see what you have achieved at the Priory. It is so exciting to think it is being brought alive again.

"I can remember as a child being scared to ride past

the end of the drive on my pony, even when I had a groom with me. It was always so gloomy, the windows shuttered, the doors barred and the garden filled with weeds. There were rumours that it was haunted. I know I was told dreadful tales by my nursemaid. They scared me into being good."

She paused for breath before she added,

"I can remember her saying that ghosts roamed the house and everyone in the nearby village was too frightened to walk past it."

Sir Michael gave a hearty laugh.

"That was true," he said, "but things have changed considerably in the last year. In fact, you can ask your cousin, Miss Allen. I think she has been most impressed by the progress I have made."

"Dulcie?" Ravina asked, intrigued. "Has Dulcie visited the Priory?"

"Oh, it was quite proper," Sir Michael said hastily. "We met in Rosbourne when I was looking for furniture and she kindly offered to bring me some samples of curtain material. With her help I chose the fabric I wanted and she arranged to have the drapes made.

"I was most grateful to her, and I am sure she will confirm that it would be perfectly safe for you to visit the parts that have been fully restored."

Ravina tossed her head.

"Oh, well, I am quite certain that I am far braver than Dulcie. If I came to see the Priory, then I would want to see it all, not just the safe areas."

Sir Michael smiled at her enthusiasm. She was certainly a very different female to her quiet older cousin.

"Perhaps you will have some ideas for the rooms that I have not yet touched," he suggested. "Miss Allen – "

"I certainly have more up-to-date ideas than Dulcie,"

Ravina cut in scathingly. "I will be only too pleased to help you."

"I wonder – " Sir Michael walked to the window, then turned to face her again, but she could not see the expression on his face because the light came from behind him.

"If you are leaving tomorrow for the country, perhaps you could assist me by allowing me to accompany you? I had intended to drive down, but my motor car has developed a very strange clanking noise under the bonnet and the mechanic tells me it will take a few days to repair."

Ravina was rather surprised at his proposal. At the same time, she felt it would be unnecessarily rude to say that she preferred to travel alone.

"Of course," she agreed, after a moment's pause. "I will be delighted to convey you to Dorset. But I intend to leave very early tomorrow. Before breakfast, in fact. Perhaps you would find that too much of a rush?"

"On the contrary, it would suit me very well. I am most obliged."

Ravina rang the bell for Gibbs.

"Then I will see you in the morning, Sir Michael, and we can tackle the Priory together."

She hesitated as she spoke, realising that perhaps she was being too forward.

Then she shrugged. Surely no one could disapprove of her helping a neighbour decorate his home. What harm could there be in that?

Gibbs appeared and ushered Sir Michael from the room. Ravina heard them walking across the hall, the sound of the front door opening and closing and Gibbs's footsteps echoing back down the passage.

Just then she realised that her visitor had left his gloves on a chair. She picked them up and ran swiftly to the front door.

She heaved it open and peered out to see if Sir Michael was still in view. But he was not.

Then to her surprise, as she stood on the top step, the gentle wind blowing her skirt into a flurry around her ankles, she realised that a tall cloaked figure was walking past.

It was the rude stranger again. The one from the ball. As she gasped, he looked up, his dark eyes seeming to burn into hers.

He raised his hand in a sombre salute and walked past, vanishing round the bend of the Crescent as if he had never been there at all.

CHAPTER THREE

Ravina spent a restless night, tossing and turning in her pink and gold bedroom, her dreams haunted by the stranger's dark piercing gaze.

She rose at dawn, hours earlier than usual, feeling weary and irritable and was bathed, dressed and downstairs before the housemaids had finished sweeping the gleaming staircase.

They looked astonished to see her up and about, but Ravina was too engrossed in her own thoughts to notice their expressions.

She had seen the dark-haired man three times now. Surely it could not be a coincidence?

She had heard of men stalking their victims – indeed, one of her friends had undergone a very distressing experience with a young curate, who had pressed his attentions on her daily, even lurking in the shrubbery in her garden to spy on her.

Admittedly the poor young clergyman had been found lacking in his brain and was now receiving treatment in a mental hospital, but it showed Ravina that strange events could occur in even the most sheltered of lives.

Could the man she had seen three times be someone similar? Surely not. There had been no sign of weakness in his face. All she had seen was determination and strength.

Within minutes all the hustle and bustle of a household in the throes of moving erupted around Ravina.

Trunks and boxes were loaded onto the second carriage and the servants who were going down to the country climbed aboard, chattering happily and glad of this break to their routine.

Splendidly attired in her best black outfit, her Sunday bonnet adorned with a wreath of cherries, Nanny Johnson made her way slowly downstairs, grumbling under her breath.

Ravina hurried across the hall to slip a hand under her arm, but the old lady shook it off.

"Now, now, Lady Ravina. There's no need to play the nurse with me. I may be old, but I'm not decrepit! Now, are you sure about travelling to Dorset alone with this Sir Michael Moore? I think young Charity should be in the carriage as well. And why are you ruining your hands driving the team when George can do it perfectly well?"

"Oh, Nanny, don't fuss so," Ravina exclaimed, laughing happily, helping her into the carriage and making sure she had a thick rug tucked round her knees.

"I am handling the horses because I love driving and George will be ready to take over the reins if I need a rest."

Just then Sir Michael arrived by Hackney cab and stood watching as the heavily laden staff coach trundled away down the road.

"You are certainly travelling light, Sir Michael," Ravina commented as he was only holding a small leather valise.

"Unlike you ladies, I do not need quite so many changes of outfit and I have most of my country clothes at the Priory already. When my car has been repaired, Goodwin, my chauffeur, will drive it down with the rest of my cases."

31

"I, on the other hand," Ravina smiled, "have so many outfits to pack that I almost needed a third coach for the luggage!"

"I trust you have remembered some pretty evening dresses. I intend to give a big party when the Priory is ready for visitors."

"How long will that be?"

"Oh, not too long. But there is still a great deal to be done before I can accommodate a large number of visitors and their staff."

"You will certainly be extremely popular with the local families, Sir Michael. The last time I was in Dorset, my friends were bemoaning the fact that there were too few parties to attend."

With a clatter of hooves and grating of wheels on the roadway, a smaller carriage emblazoned with the Ashley crest on its side panel and pulled by two beautiful greys, came round the corner.

George Jarvis, the elderly coachman, jumped down from the driving seat to hold the horses' heads, while, with a disapproving frown, the footman helped Ravina to take his place, pulling a warm rug over her knees.

Sir Michael stared in disbelief as he cautiously climbed up to sit beside her.

Ravina raised her hand in farewell to the servants who were standing in the doorway, then released the brake and shook up the reins, guiding the team into a slow controlled walk as George leapt onto the little seat behind her.

She realised Sir Michael was looking at her in astonishment.

"I know you did not expect it to be me driving the carriage today," she said mischievously, "but it is what I enjoy more than anything. It was remiss of me not to mention it yesterday."

"I am very impressed," Sir Michael told her. "But it does surprise me that you like driving a carriage and pair in London with all the traffic."

"Oh, I have done it for years," Ravina replied, exaggerating slightly. "Papa always said that if I had been a boy, I would have learnt to drive. Being a girl should not stop someone doing what they want to do, don't you agree?"

Sir Michael muttered something vague and Ravina tried not to giggle as she saw his knuckles were white where he was gripping the edge of his seat.

She flicked her whip at the ear of the offside horse to keep his head straight and smiled swiftly at her companion.

"Sir Michael, I first rode to hounds when I was five and was taught to drive almost as soon as I could hold the reins. Believe me, you are quite safe in my hands."

"Well, Lady Ravina, you have certainly surprised me this morning."

"I promise you that we will indeed arrive quite safely in the country. And, to put your mind completely at rest George is ready and eager to leap to my aid if I encounter any problems I cannot deal with."

"The way you handle the team tells me that there is unlikely to be anything that you could not overcome. Indeed, you seem like a young Queen Boadicea, riding her chariot into battle!"

Ravina laughed. She was pleased by the compliment, even if she found it a little too flowery for her taste.

She glanced sideways at Sir Michael, ready to return the compliment with some silly remark about conquering armies, when she realised the expression on his face was far from light-hearted.

He was gazing at her with a very warm look in his eyes and for an instant or two she remembered that this man was indeed almost a complete stranger.

"If you continue to make such remarks, I shall have to ask George to take over the reins," she said. "I cannot blush and drive at the same time, Sir Michael!"

"Then I will keep my compliments until later."

Ravina grinned and turned back to her task.

"We all enjoy compliments, but do tell me more about the Priory," she asked swiftly, trying to bring the conversation back onto neutral ground.

"I fear my words will not do it justice. It is an extremely old edifice. It was, as its name suggests, once a religious building, but it has been in disrepair for many years. I am pleased with the progress I have made with its restoration and I shall await your verdict with great anticipation.

"In fact, I have been thinking, Lady Ravina. I intend to hold a house warming ball in the near future for the whole County, and, as I told you yesterday, I will be giving a little dinner party for close neighbours earlier.

"I shall need some female guidance and someone to play the hostess for the evening. What do you say to the idea of coming to stay at the Priory so that you can be on hand to supervise the arrangements? I beg of you to be my guest, even if it is only for two or three nights."

Ravina felt a frisson of excitement. She had never been in sole charge at a dinner party. Her mother had obviously always been present to oversee everything with her calming presence.

"I would enjoy such a prospect a great deal," she said, her blue eyes sparkling. "I have lots of ideas on how to make a social occasion go well. And I am extremely keen on seeing what you have done to the Priory and how I might help you."

Sir Michael regarded the softness of her cheek and the full but determined curve of her mouth. He had never encountered anyone with such enthusiasm for life.

Ravina was unlike any other lady he had ever met. There was a boldness to her manner, which many men might find unappealing, but he found it invigorating.

"I shall certainly be interested to hear your views," he responded. "I was keen to have your father's advice on my racehorses, but yours will be just as welcome. I want the Priory to be as fine and beautiful a residence as when it was first built."

Ravina gave a cry and her fingers tightened on the reins, causing the horses to falter slightly. She grimaced in annoyance with herself, knowing that her emotions had travelled down the reins to their sensitive mouths.

"I am nowhere near as clever as my father. Perhaps you would be better advised to wait until he and Mama return from their travels to the Balkans."

"I think you will be exactly what my house requires," Sir Michael intoned gravely and watched as the colour flooded into her cheeks.

They drove for a long way in silence. Ravina was only too aware that his gaze was constantly on her face and although she was flattered by his attention – indeed what girl would not enjoy having the admiration of such a gentleman – she still felt slightly uneasy and was not quite sure why.

After two hours driving, Sir Michael suggested that they stopped at a hotel in a small country town to rest the horses and stretch their limbs.

Ravina was only too glad to do so. She enjoyed driving, but her close proximity to Sir Michael was making her feel uncomfortable.

Although he had behaved like a perfect gentleman, she still wished now that she had told him there was no room in the coach for him.

35

Leaving George in charge of the horses, they entered the hotel.

It was a busy bustling place and the foyer was a hive of activity with people coming and going, piles of luggage awaiting transport, porters and messenger boys criss-crossing the floor with dizzying speed.

Leading off the well-appointed dining room was a pleasant conservatory full of beautiful begonias and potted tropical plants of every shape and colour.

Pretty white and green striped chairs were gathered around wicker tables and Ravina sank back against the cushions, glad to be free of the carriage for a while.

Coffee and almond biscuits were brought in by a smiling waitress and Ravina admired the patterns made on the floor by petals falling from a huge golden flower.

Sir Michael followed her gaze and frowned,

"What a mess that plant has made. Shall I ask for the floor to be swept, Lady Ravina? I am surprised that an establishment of this class cannot keep its public rooms tidier."

Ravina stared at him, startled, then lowered her eyes and murmured something non-committal under her breath. She had suspected he was joking, but it was obvious from his expression that he was deadly serious.

'Goodness, how pompous can you be?' she thought. 'A few flower petals hardly constitute chaos.'

And she felt a twinge of regret. For all his charming manners and compliments, Sir Michael suddenly seemed a little old and stuffy.

'But he is educated and charming,' she scolded herself. 'Perhaps it is my views that are unschooled and undisciplined.'

Feeling guilty, she tried extra hard to be attentive to Sir

Michael, who was telling her the history of hothouse plants and listing in alphabetical order the varieties that he would grow at the Priory when his greenhouses were in full working order.

"When you come to stay for a few nights, you will see exactly what I have planned," he said, smiling warmly at her. "I am a great believer in order. I insist that my gardeners group all the plants together by colour and size. I dislike gardens where red and pink and purple are allowed to intermingle indiscriminately."

"I shall look forward to it immensely," Ravina replied faintly. "I am sure I shall be most impressed."

And she crossed her fingers silently under her napkin as she spoke – a childish habit she had never quite grown out of when she told a little lie.

At last, with the coffee drunk, Ravina felt she had smiled and complimented Sir Michael enough and that it was time to continue their journey.

"I will pay our bill," Sir Michael said, looking around for the waitress who was nowhere to be seen.

With an irritated exclamation about inefficiency, he hurried out of the conservatory and Ravina rose, smoothing down the skirt of her blue travelling suit.

She could hear water running prettily somewhere close by and wandered round to the back of the flowers to find a small indoor fountain and then –

"Oh!"

A man was sitting in a chair on the other side of the display, his long legs stretched out in front of him.

His tanned hand shot out to grasp her wrist as she almost fell over his feet.

Ravina was laughing as she raised her eyes to his face and then gulped.

It was the same dark-haired man again.

"Sir! Are you following me?"

Deep brown eyes looked at her as he slowly stood up, a tall slim man with a strong handsome face.

"If I have the misfortune to be in your vicinity when you are playing the flirt, madam, I assure you that it is not by choice."

Ravina started. She had not been flirting with Sir Michael!

Well, maybe a little, she conceded, her innate honesty coming to the surface, but only because he had been kind and she was guilty at feeling bored by his conversation.

"Eavesdropping is not a very gentlemanly action, sir. May I know who it is whom I have so offended by my behaviour?" she snapped.

The stranger bowed briefly.

"Sir Richard Crawford at your service."

"I am Lady Ravina Ashley and I find it strange, sir, that we should meet in this fashion."

Sir Richard shrugged.

"Life is full of little coincidences. I am sure we would find we have acquaintances in common and this hotel is the obvious place to stop for refreshment when one is heading for Dorset from London."

Ravina bit her lip.

Everything he said was true, but that did not explain his presence on horseback outside her house the night before or the fact that he had been walking past on foot later.

Meeting twice she could perhaps accept as a coincidence, but not four times.

"So, what would your parents think of your staying overnight at Sir Michael Moore's house?"

Ravina felt angry. What right had this man to ask her such a question?

"That is none of your business, sir!" she exclaimed.

"I think it is everyone's business when a young lady seems to be placing herself in a situation that could be easily misconstrued by Society gossips."

He stood up and Ravina was tempted to take a step backwards. He seemed to tower over her, intimidating her with his dark eyes. But she refused to be cowed.

She raised her chin in a stubborn gesture that her parents would have recognised only too well. Everyone who had watched Ravina growing up knew that she could be led, but never pushed.

"I am quite capable of making my own decisions about my friendships," she said, her blue eyes blazing. "We are not living in the last century when women were not allowed to have opinions of their own. I do not need any guidance from anyone – least of all a perfect stranger."

Sir Richard's lips tightened into a thin white line.

"Flirting with a gentleman who has just asked you to spend a few nights under his roof tells me that you need all the guidance you can get."

Ravina felt her temper rising. She opened her mouth to snap a sharp reply, but heard voices from the other side of the room. Sir Michael was returning with the waitress.

There was no time to tell Sir Richard exactly what she thought of him.

She dropped the merest hint of a curtsy, turned on her heel and walked away, head high, blinking back the tears that were now threatening to fall.

How dare he say such things about her. Why, he made it sound as if she was some flighty flibbertigibbet with no morals and no sense of how to behave.

She could not remember when she had been so upset

and angry.

Leaving the hotel, Ravina returned to her carriage feeling hot and flustered.

George was waiting to hand her up into the driver's seat when common sense took over.

She knew she was in no fit state to drive carefully. From the first day her father had allowed her to handle a horse in harness, the rules had been plain – you never allow the animals or your passengers to come to grief because of how you are feeling. All your decisions had to be made with a clear head and at the moment hers was far from that.

"Lady Ravina – " George said hesitantly.

"Yes, George?"

"I thought you should know, when I was at the stables, I was approached by a man askin' if this was the Ashley carriage and if you was travellin' in it."

"A gentleman? A friend of mine, perhaps?"

George shook his head.

"No, Lady Ravina, he were a servant – perhaps a footman. Seemed desperate keen to know who was travellin' down to Dorset from Ashley House."

"Did you tell him?"

He looked shocked.

"Certainly not, my Lady. Lord Ashley is always most insistent that we say nothin' to no one about the family's business."

"Perhaps he is from a newspaper. Sometimes they write articles about Papa and what he is doing. He may have been a reporter wanting Papa's comments on some foreign story."

She dismissed it from her mind and told George that she would let him drive the rest of the way to Dorset.

She climbed inside the coach and a few minutes later

Sir Michael joined her.

He seemed eager to talk, but Ravina suddenly felt weary of making conversation. She closed her eyes and let the swaying carriage lull her.

But her mind would not relax. All she could see were Sir Richard Crawford's dark angry eyes.

All she could hear was the ringing accusation in his voice – that she was flirting unwisely with Sir Michael and that her parents would be appalled.

'Oh, odious man!' she thought. 'At least Sir Michael has been nothing but charming to me all the way from London. He might be a bit boring, but at least he has the manners of a *gentleman*.'

At long last, Ravina could tell by the slowing of the horses that they had reached their destination. She opened her eyes to find Sir Michael gazing eagerly from the window.

"Ah, Lady Ravina, we have arrived at the Priory. May I impose on you to have your first look and tell me what you think?"

Ravina pulled up the blind and looked out.

The horses were walking slowly up a long straight drive laid out with formal gardens on each side.

In front of them was the old stone house, its walls covered with a bright red creeper that had been pruned back neatly from the mullioned windows.

Even from a distance, Ravina could see that the whole place gave the appearance of being repaired and restored.

A fine new gravelled area in front of the main door had been recently raked into neat patterns. Everything looked spick and span. Even the flowerbeds were arranged neatly in rows with all the reds in one area and blues and whites in another.

"Goodness!" Ravina exclaimed. "I thought as we came down the drive that George must have driven to the wrong house.

"I remember often peeping through the gates of the Priory when I was young. The drive was always overgrown with tall weeds and the house looked run down, almost a ruin. Now look at it. Anyone would be delighted to call it home."

Sir Michael laughed with pleasure, his rugged face appearing much younger.

"You are saying exactly the right things, Lady Ravina," he told her. "I will be very hurt if you do not come over for lunch tomorrow, because I have a thousand questions to ask you and frankly I shall find it impossible to do any more to the house until I have sought your help and advice."

"Thank you, but I am sure my help will not be needed, although I am complimented that you think it will."

"And you will stay for a few nights soon? We have plenty of rooms. I am sure your cousin will come too so you would be well chaperoned."

Ravina nodded and smiled sweetly, but did not reply.

She had forgotten Dulcie. But of course, she could go with her to the Priory.

That wretched Sir Richard Crawford could not have been more wrong. If she was well chaperoned, there would be no reason for her not to stay at the Priory.

Sir Michael jumped down from the carriage when they arrived and with many more warm words of thanks, stood waving as George turned the carriage and shook the horses into a trot.

Ravina sat back with a sigh. In fifteen minutes they would reach Curbishley Hall. She was longing for a nice cup of tea and the comfort of her own room.

George swung the team out of the gates and flicked the

whip to urge them on. It was uphill for a few miles and the team was tired and needed all his attention.

That was a pity because if he had glanced behind him, he would have noticed a man riding a foam-flecked horse, standing hidden behind a clump of bushes.

The same man who had spoken to him in the courtyard of the hotel at lunchtime.

But even George's sharp eyes would not have picked out another shape – a solitary grey horse and rider, outlined for a second against the crest of a rise before they merged into the trees and vanished from view.

CHAPTER FOUR

Ravina's irritation vanished like an early mist as the coach finally crested the last hill and began the long run down towards Curbishley Hall.

She leant out of the window enjoying the feel of the breeze on her cheeks. She could almost believe she could taste salt from the sea in the air.

She pulled off her hat and let the wind tease her blonde hair out of its tightly bound coils.

There. They were almost home.

Curbishley Hall, the Earl of Ashley's country seat, lay in a wide valley, sheltered from the sea on one side by rolling hills and from the nearby town of Rosbourne by a great track of woodland.

It was a splendid house, gleaming softly golden in the late evening sun and surrounded by beautiful grounds and gardens.

Ravina could tell from all the activity outside the beautiful porticoed front door that the servants' coach had arrived.

She could see Nanny Johnson being helped up the steps by a footman. By rights she should have gone to the servants' entrance with the others, but no one would dare say so to the old lady, especially not Ravina.

"Ravina, my dear – how lovely to see you again. It has been too long."

Dulcie came running down the front steps to greet her – a tall, thin, dark-haired woman wearing a dark blue dress, cut very severely with only slight touches of white lace at her collar and cuffs.

The thin chain belt around her waist carried all the various keys and necessities of her role as housekeeper.

Although she was only twenty-eight, her recent troubled life had left its mark. There were a few premature grey hairs and a small frown constantly marred her pleasant kindly features.

Two years previously, on the sudden death of her father, Dulcie had been left alone and destitute.

She was deeply grateful to Lord Ashley for rescuing her from a life of poverty and establishing her at the Hall, where she now had a home and a small income.

"Dulcie. Oh, I am so glad to be here. You are looking very well."

"You are late. I was beginning to worry. Did you have trouble with the carriage?"

Ravina slipped her arm through her cousin's as they mounted the steps to the front door.

"Oh, no. The journey was quite uneventful."

She stood for a long moment as she entered the hall, taking in with renewed pleasure the polished parquet floor and the great staircase.

Deep bowls of blue and white china full of heavy headed roses stood on small inlaid tables. A familiar scent hung in the air, telling Ravina that she was indeed home once more.

"My dear Dulcie, I must tell you – such a joke – I was late because I had a passenger. I was bringing Sir Michael

45

Moore down from London to the Priory."

Dulcie turned to tidy away a few rose petals that had fallen from a vase.

"Sir Michael is back home again, is he? That is good news for the district. He is much admired locally for all his good works for the poor of the County. But was it wise for you to travel with him on your own, Ravina? You know how people talk."

Ravina tossed her head.

"Oh, people. What do I care about people? Anyway, it was all very proper. Goodness, we had George with us all the way down and stopped for refreshment at a large hotel. Nothing could have been more refined."

She pushed away the memory of Sir Richard Crawford's sarcastic comments about her behaviour. Dulcie definitely did not need to know about that particular meeting!

"Anyway, I like Sir Michael. He has asked me to go over to the Priory for lunch tomorrow and advise about his restoration ideas before he throws a ball. I admit I am quite looking forward to helping him."

Dulcie looked up startled, biting her lip.

"He wants you to – ?"

She stopped, as if lost for words, before continuing,

"Well, I am sure you will have lots of modern London ideas to suggest. I have met Sir Michael in Rosbourne and he mentioned that he is eager to restore the Priory to its former glory.

"Indeed, I did venture to show him some samples of furnishing fabrics and found him a seamstress to make some curtains, but obviously, I have no idea of modern trends. No idea at all."

She walked across to the stairs, before turning back to Ravina.

"I have asked for a light supper to be served for you. You must be hungry, but you would not sleep following a heavy meal."

"Will you join me?" Ravina asked.

Although Dulcie was the housekeeper, she was still treated as family by the Ashleys and always ate with them when they were in residence.

"No, if you will excuse me, I must check with the maids that all is in order upstairs. And I have to try to keep the peace between Mrs. Crandle and our Mrs. Diver. Two cooks in one kitchen is never an easy situation!"

"Do you like Sir Michael?" Ravina asked as her cousin turned away.

Dulcie stopped, rubbing her hand along the polished banister as if searching for dust.

"I do not know him well, but he seems a well-informed gentleman. Very polite.

"As I mentioned, I did venture to take some samples over to the Priory and he liked them, so I ordered some curtains made. I expect he was only being polite. I have no doubt he will take them down very soon.

"Indeed, our country tastes will seem extremely out of date to you and him. Well, Ravina, I am so pleased you are here. I will look forward to hearing all your news in the morning when you have rested."

Ravina watched as the slim figure in the plain blue dress vanished up the stairs.

She felt from her tone that Dulcie did not approve of Sir Michael.

Well, that was unfortunate as she fully intended to take him up on his offer to stay at the Priory for a few days, regardless of what Cousin Dulcie and the wretched Sir Richard Crawford thought.

She ran upstairs to her room to tidy her windblown hair, but half way there, gave an irritated exclamation.

She had left her reticule in the carriage tucked under the seat.

She debated sending one of the footmen to find it, but decided it would be far quicker and easier to go herself.

Dusk had fallen swiftly while she had been indoors, but Ravina had spent half of every year of her life at Curbishley Hall and she knew all the paths and gates leading to the stable block.

She retrieved her bag and started back towards the house along a side path through the rose garden.

She stopped to pull down a large swag of white roses from a climbing bush and broke one off to wear in her hair.

Then she hesitated, looking around her.

She had the oddest feeling that someone was standing just behind the big wooden arbour, watching her.

"Hello. Who's there?" she called.

She felt no fear. Indeed, it had been a long time since she had been afraid of anything, but it was a little odd. If it was a member of the staff, why did they not show themselves?

Unless, of course, she thought suddenly, it was someone who should have been on duty and not wasting time in the rose garden.

Someone, perhaps, who knew Dulcie had retired for the evening and was taking advantage of her absence.

Ravina bit her lip. She did not want to get anyone into trouble. Maybe one of the footmen and one of the maids were courting. There was nowhere indoors where a man and a girl could speak privately.

Indeed, she knew that Dulcie would have no compunction in dismissing any servant whom she considered less than efficient.

Ravina turned and quickened her pace to bring her once again to the front of the house. Whoever it was would have a chance of returning to work by slipping indoors through the scullery.

As she rounded the corner of the house, she stopped abruptly.

A man leading a grey horse was walking up the drive.

And even in the half-light of the summer evening, Ravina could see that the man was Sir Richard Crawford!

"Sir Richard?" she snorted, crushing the white rose between her fingers, the petals floating to the ground.

"Lady Ravina."

He bowed and just then someone began turning up the lamps in the house, and she could see in the light streaming from the windows that he looked tired and drawn and that his horse was sweating and covered with mud from heavy riding.

"I must apologise for my untimely arrival. My stallion has gone somewhat lame, otherwise I should have been here earlier. If it is not too much trouble, I should like to speak to your father."

Ravina became aware of a footman running down the stone steps towards them.

She hesitated. She knew what she must do, but she really did not want to do it.

"Please come in, Sir Richard," she said at last. "I am afraid my parents are not here, but I can offer you some refreshment while one of my men tends to your mount."

She gave instructions for the horse to be taken to the stables and walked into the house, aware that Sir Richard was following closely behind her.

In the small drawing room, she rang for Gibbs and

stood hands folded in front of her.

Sir Richard did not speak and they stood in uneasy silence until the butler appeared.

"Gibbs, Sir Richard Crawford has arrived. His horse has gone lame. I am sure he would appreciate a drink."

"Just coffee, please," Sir Richard said.

"And could you please inform Miss Allen that we have a visitor, but she need not come down if she has already retired."

"Certainly, my Lady."

"Do sit down, Sir Richard. You make me feel quite nervous."

Dark eyes gleamed from his tanned face and his lips twitched in what might have been a smile as he flicked up the tails of his dark green riding jacket and sank onto a hard backed chair.

Ravina sat on a sofa, as far away from him as was politely possible.

"I find it hard to believe that anyone could make you feel nervous, Lady Ravina," he said and for an instant she thought he was laughing at her.

"Men do not suffer from nerves, sir," she retorted. "So I see no reason for women to do otherwise."

He nodded and continued to observe her.

Ravina frowned.

The familiar sense of irritation his presence caused her was beginning to make itself felt once more.

"My father is out of the country, sir," she began when the silence had gone on long enough. "It is a great pity you did not mention the reason for your journey to Dorset when we met at the hotel today.

"I could have saved you the time and trouble to yourself and your poor horse. Indeed, you must have ridden him extremely hard to have arrived here when you did. He looked quite exhausted."

Sir Richard could hear the note of disapproval in her voice that she did nothing to hide.

"He is well used to hard travelling, Lady Ravina. A few days rest and his leg will be as good as new."

He bent to flick some dust from the edge of his jacket and murmured,

"I was not aware that Lord Ashley was out of the country. He must have left quite recently."

"Indeed. My parents are holidaying in the Balkans."

She was not going to mention the real reason for her father's trip. That he was journeying on Foreign Office affairs was no one's business but his.

"Leaving you on your own?"

Ravina sighed.

"Are we to have another conversation where you warn me about my riotous behaviour?"

Sir Richard shrugged and was about to speak when a footman arrived with the coffee on a silver salver.

Ravina noticed that he drank it black with no sugar and then was annoyed with herself for bothering to watch what he did.

The thin porcelain cup looked small in his lean tanned hand. It was obvious from his appearance that he had been abroad quite recently and she wondered where.

"I have the utmost respect for Lord Ashley. Far be it for me to question your parents' decisions regarding you in any way. I just feel that a young lady should be aware that everything she does and says in public plays a part in how she is perceived by the world at large. Sometimes an older, wiser head can divert trouble before it occurs."

"So you believe I am incapable of making correct

decisions for myself?"

Ravina found she was beginning to get annoyed all over again. This man was so infuriating. He treated her as if she was ten – no six!

Sir Richard carefully placed his coffee cup back on the tray.

He was deeply worried that Lady Ravina was on her own, here in the depths of Dorset. But he did not want to scare her, just make her a little more aware that you could not trust everyone you met.

She stood up and walked over to him.

"I suppose you are one of those old-fashioned men who think a husband should make every decision in a family and that his wife should just nod sweetly and agree, even if she thinks he is wrong."

His dark eyes suddenly looked unhappy and his mouth tightened.

"I am not in a position to judge family life as such, ma'am."

There was a silence again before Ravina asked,

"You wished to see my father? May I enquire the nature of your business? Can I give him a message or help in some way?"

Sir Richard stood up and she was aware again of how tall he was.

"I met Lord Ashley when we were both in Greece. He mentioned the beauty of the Dorset countryside and suggested I call on him when I returned to England. He knew I would be in the market for an estate as I wish to breed horses and he said he would give me any advice he could."

Ravina stared at him, unsure of what to say.

'Goodness,' she thought, 'everyone seems to be moving to Dorset!'

She wondered which property her father had been thinking about.

"So if you can think of any large comfortable houses around this neighbourhood – with enough ground for horses, I would be grateful for your help."

Sir Richard leant his arm against the marble mantelpiece and stared down at her.

"Indeed, a house similar to that owned by the man who travelled with you today would be exactly right. Perhaps he would be willing to sell it to me? As you are obviously great friends, what do you think?"

Ravina became aware that colour was flooding into her cheeks.

"Sir Michael is not a 'great friend' of mine, sir. He is a kind and attentive acquaintance and a near neighbour. I have no idea of his future plans, but I think from all he has told me, that he will never sell the Priory."

"Then I shall have to look elsewhere, will I not?"

For a second, Ravina thought she detected a twinkle of amusement in Sir Richard's dark eyes, but then chided herself for being fanciful.

She had been sure that he was the type of man she detested the most – one who had no sense of humour whatsoever.

"I will certainly ask amongst my friends in the area," she continued. "If there are any suitable properties for sale locally, someone will surely know."

Sir Richard bowed gravely.

"You have my thanks, Lady Ravina. And now – " he pulled a slim gold watch from his waistcoat pocket, "I have another favour to ask. As my horse is lame, I would be grateful to stay the night here at Curbishley Hall. I could, of course, make my way to the local hostelry, but – "

Ravina hesitated.

She was certain that if her parents had been at home, they would have offered him all the hospitality for which they were famous.

But was it proper for her to have a strange man staying in the house, even though she was, of course, well chaperoned by Dulcie and all the staff?

She took a deep breath. She was being old-fashioned. She who prided herself on being as modern and up-to-date as possible. In this day and age she could surely make her own decisions.

"Of course not, sir. My parents would be shocked to hear that you had been turned away. I will arrange for a room to be made ready for you at once."

Sir Richard bowed again and watched as Ravina rang for Gibbs and gave him the necessary instructions.

He was more than thankful that she had given in to her more impulsive nature and allowed him to stay. For a moment he had been worried in case a more mature Lady Ravina had surfaced and he had been forced to leave.

It was imperative that he stayed in the house this evening. She was in great danger, but he was not sure from which direction it would strike.

But strike it would. The stakes were too great.

He cursed silently that he had no name to put behind the rumours that had sent him on this difficult and delicate mission.

Ravina left Sir Richard to Gibbs, ran up the stairs and tapped on Dulcie's door.

"Dulcie. Are you awake? I need to speak to you."

There was a rustling and the door opened a crack to reveal Dulcie, wrapped in her long dressing-gown, her hair twirled up inside a soft cotton sleeping cap.

"Ravina. Whatever is wrong? Is there a fire?"

"No, of course not. I am so sorry to waken you, but I just wanted to let you know that Sir Richard Crawford is staying the night."

"What? Gibbs told me that he had just called to see your father?"

"Yes, he did, but his horse is lame and I cannot send him away to spend the night at the *Blue Boar* in Rosbourne. Father would be furious if I did."

Dulcie clutched the collar of her gown tightly to her neck.

"Oh, dear, Ravina. I really do not feel that this is wise."

Ravina smiled and patted her cousin's arm.

"Do not fret so, Dulcie dear. Gibbs will prepare a room for him in the guest wing and I am sure he will be up and away early in the morning before we are even awake. I will leave instructions that he can stable his horse here until it recovers and take one of our mounts to carry him on his way."

She left Dulcie still murmuring her objections and slipped away to her own room where Charity helped her unpin her long blonde hair and prepare her for bed.

But when Charity had gone, Ravina felt too restless to sleep.

She turned off the oil lamp and pushing aside the pale blue curtains from the windows, she opened the casements to let in the soft night air.

Ravina's room was at the side of the house overlooking the gardens that swept down to the river beyond.

All was quiet and dark outside.

Nothing moved in the still night, until the crunching of gravel caught her attention and she leant further out to see a dark shape walking round the side of the house.

It was only one of the young footmen carrying a large box which Ravina recognised as one that her father had sent down from London containing a variety of provisions.

Ravina sighed. She plucked one of the small yellow roses that rambled up the wall and cascaded over her windowsill all summer long. It had a sweet, heady scent like honey.

'I wonder if Sir Richard is asleep,' she thought. It was odd to think of that tall, stern-faced man lying in bed in the other wing of the house.

'He is a strange gentleman. So severe and difficult, but sometimes there is an expression in his eyes which makes me think that under that austere surface is a person I could, perhaps, come to like.'

She fell into a deep reverie and had no idea how long she had been sitting at the window, when the gravel on the pathway beneath her crunched again and Ravina glanced down casually from her perch, expecting to see the footman again.

Then she gulped and drew back behind the curtains.

It was Sir Richard!

Wrapped in a long black cloak, he was prowling along the path and then, as if he realised the gravel was giving away his position, he stepped onto the lawn and vanished into the shadows cast by a tall beech tree.

Ravina sat watching for another half hour but Sir Richard did not reappear.

Eventually, puzzled, she climbed into bed.

'Perhaps he had felt ill and needed the fresh air. Maybe he had taken one brandy too many after I had left him in the drawing room.'

She knew several of her father's guests had often been

in the same inebriated state after formal dinners.

Ravina had learnt from her mother that you noted, but did not comment. You just pretended that nothing had happened.

She returned to her bed, snuggling down amongst the lace, lavender-scented pillows.

She wrinkled her nose. She might be able to ignore drunkenness in a stranger, but she had never seen her dear Papa the worse for drink and she knew she could never love a man who spent so much time in his cups.

And as she finally drifted off to sleep, she was glad that the next day Sir Richard Crawford would be gone.

*

Along the corridor, Dulcie was still awake. She had lit the oil lamp in her room and sat staring at her face in the dressing table mirror.

'When did I grow so old?' she murmured as she ran her fingers over her cheeks.

Even in the warm light from the lamp, she looked pale and no amount of smoothing would remove the frown line from between her brows.

She knew she had so much to be thankful for – a home, a job, food and clothing. But oh, how wearying it was to always be grateful, especially to Ravina Ashley!

Dulcie loved her cousin, but often wondered where her headstrong ways would lead her.

She pictured Ravina as she had been this evening – excited, happy, full of the joys of youth and beauty.

Ravina had never wanted for anything in her whole life. She only had to ask and it was given to her.

'And at the moment Ravina obviously likes Sir Michael,' Dulcie whispered and the light from the lamp blurred as tears filled her eyes.

She brushed them away impatiently. She was being silly. Why should Ravina not enjoy Sir Michael's company?

So what if he was considerably older than her? It would still make a good match. He was rich, she was titled and they both had social standing, loved horses and country life. What could be more suitable than a marriage between them?

Dulcie stood up wearily, blew out the lamp and climbed into bed.

She lay gazing up at the ceiling remembering the glorious day she had spent at the Priory, helping Sir Michael choose curtains for his drawing room and advising him on the pictures to be hung in the dining room.

For a few hours she had forgotten that she was Dulcie Allen, the poor relation, housekeeper and companion. She had once again been Miss Allen of the Laurels, Little Emsworthy, a girl with a loving father, a comfortable home and a future before her.

A future that had been ruined by the wicked man who had cheated her father of his money, whose name she had never known, but whose face was etched in her mind for ever.

Dulcie slid her hand up under her pillow and her fingers closed gently around a square of linen.

A gentleman's handkerchief, still ironed into a perfect square, that Sir Michael had used to remove a piece of grit from her eye on that memorable day.

And holding it close to her heart, she finally fell asleep.

CHAPTER FIVE

The following morning, Ravina rose early. Charity helped her into a pale blue dress laced through at the neck and cuffs with dark sapphire ribbons.

Holding back her cascading curls with another length of dark blue velvet, she finished off with small blue leather slippers.

As she walked along the corridor leading to the wide staircase, she felt happy and full of the joys a beautiful summer day can bring.

Ravina was looking forward to her breakfast and anxious to see Dulcie to arrange her visit to the Priory for lunch with Sir Michael.

Would she stay there for a few nights as he had requested?

No, she felt that would not be prudent. Her parents expected her to be here at Curbishley Hall in case there were any emergencies on the estate that only her word as an Ashley could resolve.

As she reached the stairs, she paused. She could hear voices from the hall below and stopped to peer over the banister.

To her astonishment, Sir Richard Crawford was standing talking to Nanny Johnson!

Whatever he was saying, the old lady was listening,

nodding and obviously replying, reaching up to pat his shoulder as she spoke.

As Ravina watched, the tall dark man put his hand under the old lady's arm and assisted her across the hall towards the long corridor that ran towards the baize door leading to the servants' quarters.

As they passed under the stairway, she could hear Sir Richard laughing and the throaty cackle of Nanny's reply.

Ravina picked up her skirts and swiftly ran down the stairs. What could her nanny have to say to Sir Richard?

That was the first time Ravina had heard him laugh.

It made her feel odd to see his stern face soften into such a pleasant expression.

She caught up with Nanny just as she was sitting herself down at the kitchen table, ready for her breakfast.

Ravina knelt at her side.

"Nanny, dear, how are you this morning?"

The old lady's sharp dark eyes gleamed.

"Get up off the floor at once, Lady Ravina. You'll make that dress dirty and I certainly did not bring you up to behave in such a rumbustious fashion."

Ravina stood up and waved away the hovering figure of Mrs. Diver.

"I see you have met our house guest, Nanny. I saw you talking to Sir Richard in the hall. I hope he did not have any complaints about his room."

"No, he said he slept well. He seems a very nice gentleman. Looking for a house in Dorset, he told me. To breed horses."

"Yes, so I believe."

Nanny Johnson sipped her tea with a noisy slurp.

"I heard last night that Stanton Grange is to be sold.

Old Lord Stanton died last month and his heir lives in the Highlands of Scotland and does not need a house in the South."

"Stanton Grange! Goodness, Nanny. It is a horrid house. You can smell damp in the bedrooms, the kitchens have very little windows and the stabling is dreadful. Did you tell Sir Richard that it was available?"

Nanny Johnson pulled a large bowl of porridge towards her and poured a generous helping of honey over it.

"Well, I don't rightly remember. Dear, dear, my memory isn't as good as it used to be. Perhaps you had best tell him yourself, seeing as how you seem to be concerned about the type of house he purchases."

She took a large spoonful of oats and mumbled her enjoyment at the taste and Ravina knew their conversation was over.

She was drinking her hot chocolate when Sir Richard entered the breakfast room.

He bowed and took a seat opposite her, pouring himself a cup of coffee from the silver jug on the table, waving away the parlour maid's offer of help.

"Good morning, Lady Ravina. I hope that I find you well rested?"

"Good morning, Sir Richard. Yes, indeed and I trust I find you the same and that your room and bed were to your satisfaction."

"Indeed, I fell asleep immediately."

Ravina started.

She was so tempted to say, 'sir, you are a liar! I saw you outside in the grounds with my own eyes.'

But she knew, of course, that she could say nothing of the sort. Sir Richard was a guest in her parents' house and as such had to be treated with courtesy and respect.

"If you find your mount is not fully recovered, please feel free to take one of my father's horses."

Sir Richard raised a dark eyebrow at her.

"Thank you. That is a kind offer indeed. I am keen to investigate various options for buying an estate locally and without a horse, the road might be a long one."

He smiled suddenly and Ravina almost gasped at the difference it made to his severe face.

"That extremely entertaining old lady, your nanny, told me about an estate quite nearby that is now for sale. Do you know it, Lady Ravina?"

"Stanton Grange. Yes, I do."

She hesitated, toying with her fork. Should she tell him of its drawbacks or would it sound as if she was far too interested in his affairs?

"It is worth an inspection, of course, but I am sure there are lots of places that would be just as suitable."

"Wherever I look, I shall need a mount, so thank you once again for your kind offer."

"I have walked all the paths and lanes for miles around," Ravina replied. "And must admit that although the exercise is beneficial, being carried by a sturdy mount does have its advantages."

Sir Richard reached for a piece of toast and began buttering it slowly.

"Do you walk alone through the countryside?" he asked casually.

"Oh, yes, sometimes. Dulcie is always busy and Mama and Papa have no inclination for walking."

"Surely it is not entirely wise. There are all sorts of gypsies, ruffians and vagabonds roaming around these days."

Ravina laughed.

"The Romany gypsies visit Curbishley Hall every year on their travels. The men sell us pots and pans and trade working horses with Papa in exchange for other goods. I know them well and they would never harm anyone.

"I have explored every inch, every cottage and field for miles around. And it is rare that I walk far without meeting some farmer or labourer whom I have known since childhood."

Sir Richard's face had reverted to its stern expression.

He knew only too well that danger could strike at any time and that a good-natured farm lad would be scant help if it did.

This beautiful girl with her determined expression, her chin tilted so defiantly, had much courage but he knew that would be of little use in a dire situation.

"You seem, sir, to have somewhat outdated ideas of what the female of the species can do in this day and age."

The plate of toast was pushed away uneaten.

"Indeed, Lady Ravina. Young ladies feel free to do so much that they would not even have contemplated a short while ago."

Ravina pulled a face.

"Yes, you are quite right. I have heard it rumoured that some of us can even count and write our own names!"

Sir Richard's lips twitched.

"Yes, it is a dreadful state of affairs! What is the world coming to? But, joking apart, Lady Ravina, I would, in all earnestness, urge you to take very great care and not spend too much time alone far from your home."

Ravina was about to object, but stopped.

His expression was not one of cold arrogance. He seemed genuinely concerned and this puzzled her. This was not the first time he had expressed doubts about her behaviour.

Just then the door opened and Dulcie bustled in.

"Ravina, Sir Richard, please excuse me for not attending on you sooner. There has been a small revolution in the kitchen due to having two cooks in attendance. Something to do with jugged hare or rabbit pie, I believe."

Ravina stood up.

"Sir Richard, may I introduce my cousin, Miss Dulcie Allen. Dulcie, Sir Richard Crawford."

"Miss Allen. A pleasure to make your acquaintance."

"Oh, Sir Richard. Please excuse my hasty entrance," Dulcie blushed as he bowed over her hand. "I am honoured to make your acquaintance. Ravina informed me you were staying the night. I trust that everything was pleasant and comfortable?"

"It could not have been bettered in a palace," Sir Richard said gravely. "And this morning, Lady Ravina has kindly offered me the use of one of her father's horses and I am hoping that she will ride out with me to inspect some properties I am thinking of buying."

Ravina looked up, startled. He had not mentioned this idea before.

But, she thought with a secret smile, it would be fun. She did not actually like Sir Richard. He was far too opinionated for her taste, but she would like to show him the beauties of the Dorset countryside.

And, she added silently to herself, there was something secretive about the man, a puzzle that needed solving.

Why, to start with, had he been walking around outside the Hall in the dead of night?

"We could begin with Stanton Grange," she said eagerly. "It is only two miles away to the East of

Rosbourne."

"Oh, but Ravina, surely you already have an engagement? You promised to visit Sir Michael at the Priory for lunch today to discuss the alterations he is making to his home," Dulcie intervened, trying to hide her exasperation at her young cousin's lack of memory.

"Goodness, I quite forgot," Ravina exclaimed, her blue eyes wide with guilt. "I am so sorry, Sir Richard, but I have indeed promised to visit Sir Michael today. And perhaps you will be able to move a little faster around the houses without my company."

"I see. Well, if you will excuse me, Lady Ravina – Miss Allen, I must discover how my horse is this morning and then be on my way. I thank you for your hospitality and wish you both a pleasant luncheon at the Priory."

Dulcie pulled a little face, her mouth thinning.

"Oh, I shall not be going. I fear it is obvious that Sir Michael must have found my ideas for his house rather too countrified for his taste. He is anxious for Ravina's views. He is a man of such taste and dignity and I am rather ashamed to have offered my little ideas for his beautiful home."

Sir Richard frowned.

"I am sure that is not so, Miss Allen. I cannot believe that you do not have a perfect idea of what would be suitable for Sir Michael's home."

Dulcie coloured and dropped a little curtsy at his compliment.

Sir Richard bowed in return and glanced at Ravina, as if he was going to speak, then nodded and left the room.

"An interesting man," Dulcie mused. "It will be good to have him as a neighbour."

"I am sure he is most admirable and obviously Papa

65

must think so or he would not have offered him our hospitality when they met abroad. But I am afraid he has very old-fashioned views about today's women. Never a conversation passes without him lecturing me about my wayward behaviour!"

Dulcie sighed. The younger girl looked so spirited and full of life. Ravina had never known a day's trouble or problems. She believed the world was full of goodness and that bad things only happened to bad people.

Dulcie knew better. Her own father had been a dear but vague gentleman, a widower since she was born. He had lived for his books and the exotic orchids he had grown in his greenhouse and had been the bewildered victim of an unscrupulous man who had pushed him to invest all his money in non-existent stocks.

When he died, Dulcie was sure it was of a broken heart, because his belief in the goodness of his fellow man had been shattered and she would have been destitute if Lord Ashley had not offered her a place to live and a job of work to do.

But oh, how she longed for her own home once more to read the books she loved, to garden and sew and make a good home for someone dear to her.

Now she watched as Ravina left the room and ran upstairs to change into her riding clothes.

It was *Ravina* who would lunch at the Priory with Sir Michael.

Ravina who would give him advice on the restoration of his lovely old house.

Ravina who would play hostess at the ball he had promised to give for the local gentry.

Dulcie blinked away the tears that threatened to fall. She refused to allow herself to be jealous of her cousin.

After all, she had enough commonsense to realise that

a woman in her lowly position – neither a servant nor a proper family member – was not the type of person that the Sir Michaels of this world would find attractive.

But oh, how she wished her dear father had never met that dreadful man who had ruined them.

Ravina changed hurriedly into her dark amber riding costume. She fully intended to ride over to the Priory. It was too lovely a day to be shut inside a stuffy carriage.

No, she wanted to gallop across the Downs, feel the wind in her face and the freedom of being completely on her own.

She ran down the back staircase, through the side door and out to the stable block.

She had asked for Sweetie, her mare, to be saddled, but as she turned into the cobbled yard she was surprised to see a familiar figure.

His coat discarded, his fine lawn shirt rolled up above his elbows, Sir Richard was on his knees, massaging oil into his grey stallion's leg.

His hair was dishevelled, there was a smear of mud down one cheek and Ravina felt her heart give a little skip as he looked up and smiled at her.

"Why, Sir Richard, I thought you would have been long since gone," Ravina said, trying to hide her confusion.

He stood up, wiping his hands on an old piece of sacking.

"Yes, I must apologise most sincerely for still imposing on your hospitality, Lady Ravina, but I discovered that my horse did indeed need more attention. He can be a temperamental animal, as stallions often are, and I would not have wanted one of your men to be injured in dealing with him."

"Is it a bad injury?" Ravina asked, gazing with

admiration at the animal's steely grey head and dark eyes looking down at her.

"No, not at all. But one that needs tender care. I shall leave him to rest in your stables for another day, with your permission, and accept your kind offer of one of your father's mounts."

He pulled on his dark blue coat as he spoke and the boyish-looking gentleman immediately became the well dressed aristocrat.

Ravina was just about to tell him that he still had a streak of mud down one tanned cheek, when one of the grooms appeared, leading a big bay horse in one hand and Sweetie in the other.

"Oh, that is Galahad," she cried. "He is a strong and fast hunter. I am sure he will suit you perfectly."

Sir Richard swung himself into the saddle and watched gravely as she nimbly mounted and turned the mare's head towards the track that ran away across the fields.

"My route lies close to yours, I believe," he announced suddenly. "Perhaps it would be acceptable to you if we rode together?"

Ravina paused.

She had meant to gallop but knew his mount would soon outstrip hers. But he was a guest of the house and she knew her parents would expect her to treat him with all due courtesy.

"That would be pleasant," she said and together they trotted towards the woods that lay between Curbishley Hall and the Priory.

The narrow path made riding abreast difficult and Ravina pushed ahead along the mossy track.

The woods were beautiful, dark and mysterious. Occasionally she heard the sudden crack of a branch breaking and a flock of small birds burst through the undergrowth, and guessed that some deer were making their way through the dappled shade to drink at one of the lakes.

She glanced back several times and realised that Sir Richard too was obviously very intrigued by his surroundings.

His reins were quite lax in his hands and he was letting Galahad pick his own way down the track.

Sir Richard's gaze swept the woods from side to side, almost as if he was searching for something.

"You are obviously enjoying our woods, Sir Richard," Ravina called over her shoulder.

"Indeed. They are extremely fine. Good, old timber. Very dense, I see. You could hide an army in these woods and never see it. Do you always ride this way when visiting the Priory?"

"I do like to visit the woods whenever I can. I love them so much. I have seen deer, badgers, foxes – oh, and every type of bird. But, I have never actually visited the Priory before. It was in a state of disrepair for so many years when I was a child. I suppose it would be far easier to go through the village by road, but Sweetie needs the exercise."

"I see that the trees are thinning out ahead. Shall we race to the top of the hill, Lady Ravina?"

Ravina was surprised. She would never have thought that Sir Richard was the type of man to indulge in such frivolity.

But she was aching to gallop and with a chuckle she urged her mare forward.

The two horses burst out of the woods and Sir Richard sighed in relief. The heavy-leafed trees and bushes hid too much from his gaze for his liking.

He had not been joking when he mentioned hiding an army in the woods' depths.

But it was not an army of men he was worried about – but just one man! A very evil one at that.

The smooth turf of the Downs spun up under the hooves in flying clods as Ravina urged her mare on faster and faster.

This was what she loved doing – her hat had slipped down her back and her hair streamed free in the wind.

And she felt free, too. It was a marvellous sensation, escaping from the confines of Society to gallop across this beautiful country.

She could hear Galahad's heavier hooves thundering behind her, next Sir Richard was alongside and she caught a glimpse of him grinning at her as he passed her.

At the top of the hill he reined in, only seconds before she arrived.

"Well ridden, Lady Ravina!" he called, circling a snorting Galahad who was tossing his head, obviously pleased to have had such a good run.

"There are not many young ladies who could stay ahead of this beast for so long. Your mare has a good turn of speed."

Ravina smiled and tried to tidy her hair, searching for clips that were long gone in the hectic ride. She finally found a piece of blue velvet ribbon in a pocket and tied her long blonde curls back severely from her face.

"I would like to thank you, Sir Richard, for not letting me win," she said. "Many men allow women to do so and I find it so annoying. It was a fair race and you won with the faster horse."

Sir Richard's dark eyes gleamed briefly.

"It would never have crossed my mind to allow you to win," he said. "That would have been patronizing in the extreme."

"I agree, but unfortunately, most men would find your attitude ungentlemanly. They would have let me win and praised me for my ability. I know women are not as physically strong as men, but that is no reason to treat us as if we are little children."

Sir Richard had managed to calm his horse and sat, gazing down the hillside at the panorama of the English countryside spread out before them.

He loved this country with a depth of emotion that he could not put into words. Looking down at the patchwork of little fields, green, gold and brown, all neatly edged with hedges and trees, he knew he would do anything to protect it.

"But you must admit, Lady Ravina, that there are times when a young lady can find herself in a situation she cannot handle by speed and flight alone."

Ravina hesitated. It seemed to her that there was a double meaning in his words, but she had no idea what it could possibly be.

"We do have brains as well, Sir Richard. Hopefully, if it is a situation where physical prowess is not enough, then our ability to communicate will be useful and help us overcome whatever problems we face."

He smiled at her boundless optimism and, talking about a variety of subjects, they walked their horses slowly down the track towards the village.

Sir Richard was keen to know about all the Dorset landmarks and Ravina was pleased that she could point with her crop and name all the hills and valleys in sight.

In about half a mile a long stone wall marked the edge of the Priory estate, and very soon they reached the ornate black iron gates.

"Well, here we must part. I trust your search for the perfect house will be successful," Ravina said, feeling a sudden, unexpected pang of regret.

She realised that she had thoroughly enjoyed her ride with Sir Richard.

He was not the dour, critical man she had at first thought, but clever and interesting. He held views and opinions, but also listened to hers and did not insist that his were always right.

Except for his ongoing belief that women were unable to look after themselves!

Sir Richard leant across his saddle and shook her hand.

"I will take my leave of you. I hope you have a very pleasant day," he said and turning Galahad, he trotted off along the road towards the village.

Ravina watched him go. He rode so well, at one with his horse.

Sighing for no reason that she could fathom, she made her way up the drive towards the Priory and her appointment with Sir Michael Moore.

CHAPTER SIX

Trotting up the drive between the neatly laid out gardens, Ravina was once again impressed by the amount of work that had been done to the Priory to bring it back from a dilapidated state to its present glory.

Twisted chimney pots reared up against the bright blue sky. Over the years ivy and wisteria had been left to run riot over its walls, even hiding the windows and giving the building a frightening aspect from the road, especially to small children.

Even the village urchins had not dared to climb the stone walls that surrounded the immediate grounds and trespass in the orchards to scrump the fruit, even though the gnarled old trees gave copious bushel loads of apples, plums and pears every year.

The grounds had remained untouched for years, a rough wilderness for wild life. Foxes and badgers had made their home in the undergrowth. Bats had flown around the eaves and owls could always be heard at night.

Ravina could remember quite clearly a time when she had been about four or five. She had had a nursemaid, one of the village girls, Beatrice Watson, who worked under Nanny Johnson's strict regime.

Beatrice had delighted in creeping into the night nursery and telling little Ravina as she cowered under the sheets that ghosts and ghouls lived in the Priory.

She used to threaten to send her there to stay if she was naughty.

As the years passed, Ravina realised it had not been until she had told Nanny Johnson why she was so scared and having nightmares, that Beatrice had suddenly left and returned to Rosbourne to live with her brother Joe.

Now, as Ravina rode up the drive, there was nothing about the Priory that could scare any child.

All the vines had been ruthlessly cut back and trained across the walls. Rambling roses and clematis had been added to the trelliswork on the grey stones and their pale yellow and white flowers softened the austere appearance.

As Ravina arrived at the entrance, an ostler in a black and yellow uniform appeared and helped her to dismount, listening carefully to her instructions as to Sweetie's welfare following her ride.

A smartly dressed butler opened the door before she rang the bell.

"Will you come this way, my Lady. Sir Michael is waiting for you in the study."

He preceded her across a wide panelled hall, its walls hung with oil paintings of Moore ancestors and tapestries depicting ancient battles.

Two suits of armour stood on either side of the foot of the stairs. A metal arm on each was raised high in the air, one holding an axe, the other a wickedly sharp sword.

Ravina shuddered slightly. She had never cared too much for weapons and armour and these looked so lifelike.

She fancied that she could feel eyes following her across the hall.

Ravina felt that the overall effect of the entrance hall was far too dark and old-fashioned, but she did know that gentlemen did not always care for lighter colours around them.

"Lady Ravina Ashley, Sir Michael."

Ravina entered the small study which was lined from floor to ceiling with books. A huge globe stood on an ornate stand and imposing busts of ancient Greeks and Romans gazed down from niches set in the bookcases.

Ravina peered through the gloom. The heavy red velvet curtains were half drawn to keep out the sunshine and she felt a wild desire to fling open the windows, and let the country breeze wash away the overpowering smell of leather, smoke and years of male occupancy!

Dressed in dark brown country tweeds, Sir Michael rose from his desk and came towards her, his hand outstretched in greeting.

His plain but kindly face was shining with pleasure.

"Welcome, Lady Ravina. Welcome to my home. I trust I find you in good health? I was so afraid you might forget that you had promised to come and see what I have achieved here and what still needs to be done."

"How could I forget, Sir Michael? I have been looking forward to it so much," Ravina replied quickly, touching her fingers to his and pushing aside the fact that it had been Dulcie who had reminded her of today's engagement.

"And I must tell you, Sir Michael, that I am most impressed by what I have already seen. It seems to me that you have worked quite a few miracles."

"I was saddened when I first arrived and found the house had fallen into such disrepair. And I must admit to feeling proud that it is now halfway back to what a building of its age and prestige should look like."

He clapped his hands together enthusiastically and Ravina tried not to jump at the sudden noise.

"But do allow me to show you around before luncheon is served. There are many aspects on which I need a woman's advice and I am sure your artistic eye will help me see matters in a different light."

Ravina smiled and followed him out of the study. It was always pleasing to have your abilities admired.

Sir Michael led the way across the hall to a charming sunny room with French windows that opened out onto a paved terrace at the back of the house.

The proportions of the room were lovely, the furniture good and highly polished. Only the curtains and coverings of the sofas and chairs seemed dull and old-fashioned.

Ravina enthused about the size and outlook of the room, admired the furniture and made what she hoped were informed comments about the ornaments and pictures.

Then she ran her fingers down the material of the drapes at the window and turned to Sir Michael.

"Well, here is one thing I can help you with straight away – these curtains are – "

"Yes, they are extremely fine, are they not? You will probably not be surprised to learn that your cousin chose the material and found a local seamstress to make them. They change the whole aspect of the room, I think. I am so indebted to Miss Allen. As you yourself will be aware, she has extremely good taste and has been most helpful."

Ravina bit back the words 'dull and old-fashioned' before they could leave her lips.

Of course these were curtains of Dulcie's choosing. They were exactly what she would have expected her cousin to suggest. Safe and boring.

"Indeed, they do give a very – interesting depth to the room," she responded, choosing her words with great care. "Dulcie obviously shares your taste in decoration, Sir Michael."

To Ravina's surprise, a strong brick colour flooded across Sir Michael's round face.

"Miss Allen has kindly given up her valuable time to offer me some assistance in the early stages of the Priory's restoration, especially in the rooms I use the most," he murmured. "But, of course, it is the vital finishing touches in the more public rooms that are so important, are they not?

"Although, as you know, I have a small house in London, I am not *au fait* with all the latest fashions, as I am sure you are. And I am determined that when the members of our County circle come to call, they will find nothing to upset their sensibilities.

"Now, let me show you some of the rooms that still need to be reformed. The dining room, in particular, is not right. Our luncheon will soon be served there."

Ravina cast a longing glance out onto the sunny terrace. It would have been far more than pleasant to have eaten out of doors on a day such as today, but instead she obediently followed her host into the long dark dining room.

An oxtail soup that was far too hot and too thick for a summer's day was followed by a heavy steak and kidney pie, its glistening golden crust swimming in gravy.

The footman poured red wine, but Ravina did not touch it. She toyed with her food, staring in despair at the great dark oil paintings that hung on every wall.

The one directly in front of her showed a slavering wolf bringing down a poor pathetic deer during a hunt. There was a great deal of scarlet paint!

She sighed and averted her gaze. She could think of nothing more likely to put someone off their food than the sight of all that blood.

"So, Lady Ravina, do tell me, can you see how to improve this room in your mind's eye? When I hold my house-warming party, it will be in constant use and I must give the right impression to my guests."

"Perhaps some of the paintings could be moved to different locations," Ravina suggested desperately.

"Oh, do you think so?" Sir Michael took a large mouthful of steak and kidney and chewed vigorously.

"Miss Allen thought they were very fine, although she did propose that they needed to be grouped differently on the walls."

Ravina pushed her plate to one side.

She was beginning to be intrigued by his insistence on Dulcie's involvement.

Why had Sir Michael invited her, apparently for her opinion, when it was quite obvious her cousin had already been asked for her help?

"Dulcie is a dear, dear creature," she said, gratefully accepting a plate of iced fruits from the footman.

"Oh, indeed. A most refined and genteel lady. One can only be sorry for the unfortunate troubles that have left her in such distressing circumstances."

"Her father, my Papa's cousin, was sadly ill-advised with his investments."

Sir Michael took a sip of wine and frowned.

"Indeed, I believe from my conversations with your cousin that what happened could have been called a criminal offence. Am I correct, some man – I will not give him the courtesy of calling him a gentleman – blatantly lied and cheated her father out of all of his money?"

Ravina nodded. She had only met Mr. Allen and Dulcie once before their lives had changed so dramatically and that had been at a family party when she was very small.

Now she could not remember the details about Dulcie's fall into poverty. She had only been told that her cousin would be coming to Curbishley Hall as housekeeper and would be a companion for Ravina when she was in Dorset.

Obviously, Ravina had heard gossip from the servants in the weeks that followed, but Dulcie herself had said very little on the subject.

Ravina had felt it would be impolite and hurtful to ask her questions. Bringing up the past could only cause Dulcie distress and so she had not pressed her for details.

"To lose your station in life must be hard and especially so for one such as Miss Allen who has such an appreciation for the finer aspects of life. How lucky it was for her that your father stepped in to help."

"My parents would never let a family member suffer if they could possibly prevent it," Ravina replied warmly. "My father has very strong views on loyalty and duty."

"And she has told me that she will always be thankful to him."

Sir Michael cut himself a large slice of cheese and speared it with the end of his knife.

"Miss Allen owes Lord Ashley a great debt of gratitude," he continued. "I believe she would never leave, even if an offer of another position was made to her. Is that your opinion, Lady Ravina?"

Ravina looked up, startled, the melting ice sliding off her spoon and splashing onto the tablecloth.

"I cannot believe my parents would stand in Dulcie's way if, say, she was to be offered the position of housekeeper at a larger establishment – dare I even say, one of the Royal households. Although I have never heard her speak of any inclination to leave."

Sir Michael gestured to the footman who poured him another glass of wine.

"Housekeeper? Oh, yes, quite. She seems more than

happy looking after Curbishley Hall while you and your parents are in London. And of course her reduced circumstances make the possibility of changing her station in life – well, we will not continue thus. But talking of marriage, Lady Ravina – "

"Were we?" Ravina looked up, startled, wishing the footman would return with coffee to bring this awkward meal to a close.

Sir Michael pushed his plate aside and folded his hands pompously on the table in front of him.

He looked to Ravina as if he was about to preside over some official meeting.

She felt a wild desire to giggle begin to rise inside her.

"I have decided that I must turn my mind to that problem. I need a wife to provide me with an heir. The Priory needs a Mistress, someone who will care for it, help me with all the different functions I wish to give and take her rightful position in the social fabric of the County."

He took a deep breath, the buttons on his waistcoat straining.

"Lady Ravina, I know that we have – "

"Oh! Oh! Goodness me. I am so sorry!"

Ravina had jerked her hand, sending a cascade of red wine splashing across the table.

She leapt up and dabbed at her amber skirt with a linen napkin.

"Oh, dear, red wine is so difficult to remove from fabric. I do hope it will not stain. Would you ring the bell for your butler, please, Sir Michael? I know it is only a riding habit, but I must sponge it immediately."

Ravina chattered on, hardly drawing breath, glad that in the ensuing fuss, the thorny subject of marriage was forgotten.

She was also glad that she had remembered one of the many lessons Nanny Johnson had taught her.

"If you are keen for a gentleman to stop talking on a certain subject, it is far better to cause a diversion rather than try to interrupt him. Gentlemen hate to be interrupted."

A maid was summoned and escorted Ravina upstairs to a guest bedroom where she could rest while her skirt was carried away to be sponged.

Ravina lay on the bed, her head aching from the strain of the day, watching out of the window as the afternoon sun slid down the sky until it hovered above the waving green branches of the nearby woodlands.

When her skirt was finally returned to her, she lost no time in hurrying downstairs and saying her goodbyes.

Sir Michael was waiting for her in the hall. He accompanied her outside where a groom was holding Sweetie.

Ravina listened to Sir Michael's repeated promises that she and she alone should be hostess at his big house-warming party.

Hardly knowing what she was saying in her haste to leave, Ravina agreed to return in two days to finalise all the plans.

With a sense of relief she allowed the groom to help her onto Sweetie.

She gathered the reins together, waved farewell to Sir Michael and urged the mare forwards.

Then she realised the groom was still holding Sweetie's bridle, walking swiftly at her side.

"My Lady – "

"Yes – ?" Ravina peered down at the worried face. "Why, I know you! It's Bobby Watson, isn't it? Hello, Bobby, how nice to see you. I did not know you were in service with Sir Michael. I am pleased for you. This is a step-up, surely."

The Watson family were well known to Ravina and her parents. Joe Watson, the father, was a surly brute of a man who, although he was trained as a blacksmith, worked as little as possible, unless you counted poaching as work.

He feigned illness and injury and relied on the charity of nearby families to keep him and his family from the workhouse.

He lived with his wife and an ever-increasing family in a little hovel close to the river bank.

The shack was damp and dark and Ravina hated the times she was made to accompany her mother there on errands of mercy – delivering old clothes and baskets of produce to Mrs. Watson to help her cope with her brood of thin, runny-nosed children.

Ravina suddenly recalled that Beatrice, the nursemaid who had scared her so much when she was little, was Joe Watson's sister.

But Bobby, the eldest Watson boy, had always seemed to have more intelligence than the rest of his family.

Ravina knew he loved horses and she was delighted to see that he was now working in a good job. Living in at the Priory could only improve his lot. Away from the dirt and criminal tendencies of his dreadful father, he would surely make something of his life.

"Yes, my Lady. I've been here for six months now."

"I will tell my mother when she returns to England. She will be so pleased to hear that you are doing well. And how is your family?"

Bobby gazed up at her as they walked down the drive, his fingers nervously smoothing Sweetie's mane.

"They're – well, 'bout the same, I suppose, my Lady. Pa – well, he's away a lot."

Ravina was puzzled.

She did not quite understand why the boy was anxious to talk to her, but knowing how difficult it was for the whole Watson family to put together a sensible sentence, she asked,

"Is there something you want, Bobby? Something I can do for you and yours? I can arrange for my cousin, Miss Allen, to put together some supplies for your mother if she is – well, if you are expecting another brother or sister in the near future."

He licked his lips, his eyes very blue in his dirty tanned face.

"No, no, Ma is fine. We're all fine. That is, well, I want you to take care in those woods, my Lady. Don't you go ridin' out on your own."

"Bobby?"

The boy dropped the bridle as they reached the big iron gates and sidled away into the undergrowth that surrounded the gatehouse.

"I can say no more," he said, his voice sounding desperate. "Just be careful, Lady Ravina. Be careful in them there woods!"

CHAPTER SEVEN

Leaving Bobby, the Priory and Sir Michael behind her, Ravina trotted back to Curbishley Hall along the main road.

She wanted to reach home as fast as she could.

'That is the only reason I am using the road,' she firmly told herself. 'I am certainly *not* scared of the woods. Bobby is trying to frighten me with his warnings.'

She urged Sweetie into a faster trot.

'I am really disappointed in him. He is as bad as his Aunt Beatrice was all those years ago, telling me ghost stories about the Priory to punish me when I was naughty.'

She refused to pay any attention to Bobby's silly remarks. The woods, although still enticing as the sun set behind the hills, would have to wait for another day.

Once or twice, she turned in her saddle, sure she could hear hoof beats on the road behind her. But there was no sign of another horse.

To her surprise, Dulcie was in the stable yard when she rode in.

Ravina slipped from the saddle and handed the reins to the groom.

"Dulcie, were you waiting for me? Is there a problem?"

"Ravina – what – oh, no, I was just – I came down to

check – we need apples in the kitchen – Ravina, you really should not ride around the countryside on your own. It is most unwise."

"Dulcie, dearest, I was accompanied all the way to the Priory by Sir Richard and the road home was straight and quick. Whatever could happen to me in our own village?"

"And how is Sir Michael?" Dulcie asked, casually, finding great interest in the basket of fruit she was carrying. "Were you impressed by his restoration work at the Priory?"

"He seems very well. Indeed, he keeps an extremely full table for a man living on his own. If he is not careful, he might well be considered too fat in a few years' time."

Dulcie looked shocked.

"Ravina. That is a most uncharitable remark. Sir Michael is a fine figure of a man. Indeed, I know no better."

Ravina felt a mischievous smile breaking across her face and struggled to keep it back.

It was slowly becoming very clear to her exactly what Dulcie's true feelings for their near neighbour were.

But she could see that her cousin was flustered and miserable and tried to change the subject.

"Has Sir Richard returned to collect his horse?"

"No, the grooms have been waiting for him. Now it is getting dark, I imagine he has been delayed in some way. When he does arrive, we must of course, offer him our hospitality once more."

Ravina nodded, wondering why she felt such a rush of pleasure that she would be seeing the stern, dark-eyed man again.

But then, he had not seemed so stern when he was racing her across the country. She could clearly recall how he had looked when they had reined in their mounts on the top of the hill.

His dark hair had been tangled across his brow, his eyes had gleamed and the austere expression had vanished from his face.

*

If Ravina dressed for dinner with more care than usual, she refused to admit it to herself.

The cream silk dress with the lace overlay was cut lower than the ones she normally wore and she insisted that Charity tried various hair styles before she was happy with the cascade of blonde curls that fell across her shoulders from a beautiful sapphire clasp.

She was about to go down for dinner when she remembered Bobby.

Of course what he was saying was nonsense, but –

She walked upstairs to Nanny Johnson's room and found her sitting, nodding over her fire, even though the evening was warm and sultry.

Her face broke into a toothless smile as Ravina came in and sank down onto the little stool by the side of the old lady's chair – a stool she had used ever since she could remember.

"Hmm, that dress is too low cut for a country dinner, miss."

"Oh, Nanny. Don't fuss. I like it. You must try to keep up to date with the latest fashions, you know."

"Hmmph." Nanny's eyes twinkled. "The only reason I know for a young lady to wear a revealing dress when she is only dining with her companion, is that she hopes a gentleman she likes will be attending as well."

"Nanny!"

Ravina jumped to her feet and wandered round the room, fingering all the little knick-knacks that littered every inch of space.

"Did you ever want to marry and have your own family, Nanny?" Ravina asked suddenly, wondering why this was the first time this question had ever occurred to her. "Was there ever a boy you liked?"

Nanny glanced up and if Ravina had been looking in her direction, she would have seen a quick flash of something close to pain cross her old face.

She was remembering a short, stocky young man with bright brown hair and merry hazel eyes. A young man who had been swept up by the Press Gang one misty winter morning on his way to work and who had died, somewhere on the ocean, a long way away from her comforting arms, fighting for King and country.

"Far too busy looking after the Ashley children to worry about having my own," she replied. "And why are you bothering me with all these questions, Lady Ravina, when you should be downstairs enjoying the dinner the staff has laboured over preparing for you?"

Ravina smiled.

"Do you remember Beatrice Watson, Nanny?"

The old woman snorted.

"The silly chit who scared you out of the few wits you had when you were tiny? One of the Watson clan, she was."

"I saw Bobby Watson today at the Priory. He is Joe Watson's eldest boy and is working in the stables."

"Then that Sir Michael isn't the sensible man I thought he was. I wouldn't have any of the Watson clan anywhere near me."

"Bobby said – "

Nanny shushed her.

"I do not want to hear another word, Lady Ravina. Whatever he said, don't you believe it. They are all thieves and liars, those Watsons."

Ravina smiled at her old nurse's outraged expression. But she felt reassured.

Yes, it was just as she had thought.

Bobby was trying to scare her for some stupid reason of his own. She would think no more about his warning.

Leaving Nanny, Ravina felt a frisson of excitement, but when she entered the drawing room, she found Sir Richard and Dulcie deep in conversation.

Ravina was unaware of the gleam of appreciation in Sir Richard's eyes as he looked at his young hostess, although she was aware that Dulcie, wearing a neat sensible dress in green, had raised her eyebrows at her cousin's bare shoulders.

"Good evening, Lady Ravina. I trust you had an interesting day at the Priory?"

"Good evening, Sir Richard. Yes, indeed. It is a fascinating old house and Sir Michael has been most fastidious in his restoration work. And did your day go as planned? I trust your horse is now fully recovered."

"Ravina! You sound as if you are keen for Sir Richard to leave us," Dulcie said sharply.

Ravina felt the colour rush into her cheeks but Sir Richard just laughed.

"I am sure Lady Ravina has been far too busy today to give my absence a second thought. But I know you will be pleased to hear that my stallion is now back to his old self and I shall be taking my leave of you very soon."

Ravina made automatic remarks of sorrow, but inside her head, her thoughts were whirling.

He was leaving and there was no reason why they should ever meet again.

Gibbs announced that dinner was served and the three of them made their way into the dining room.

He had lit candles on the table and Ravina was aware that Sir Richard was watching her across the dancing flames as she toyed with her soup and pushed the roast chicken around her plate.

Conversation over the meal was polite and bland.

When the last dishes had been removed, Ravina led the way into the drawing room where coffee was waiting for them.

But Dulcie shook her head, saying she would never sleep if she drank coffee so late in the day and wishing them both good night, she withdrew.

Gibbs served Sir Richard with a glass of brandy, leaving the two of them alone.

The night had grown chilly and a small fire was crackling in the grate.

"Your appetite seemed poor this evening, Lady Ravina," Sir Richard commented, warming the bowl of his brandy glass between his hands. "I hope you have not overexerted yourself today. Inspecting houses that are in a state of disrepair can be tiring."

Ravina scowled.

"The majority of the building work has long been finished at the Priory," she said. "Sir Michael did not show me any area that was unsafe. It is the adornment and furnishing of the house that are his next requirements."

"And do you feel your tastes and Sir Michael's are similar?" he asked, gazing into the dancing flames.

"That is a very odd question, sir. Do you feel that one person's view of beauty differs from another's?"

"Yes, I do," he replied calmly. "Indeed, I have no doubts that my ideas of what would make a home beautiful would be far removed from Sir Michael's."

Ravina felt a flash of annoyance.

She pushed aside the memory of her distaste at the overpowering and old-fashioned atmosphere that Sir Michael was already introducing into the Priory.

"I suppose we learn first from our parents what they consider tasteful and beautiful and add our own opinions as we grow older," she said.

Sir Richard took a sip of brandy.

"I must admit that having met your father, I can only imagine that his ideas would be beyond reproach."

"That was in Greece, was it not?" Ravina asked. "Where you met?"

There was a silence for a couple of heartbeats, before Sir Richard said,

"Yes, I was there on business and happened to make your father's acquaintance. That was when he mentioned that Dorset would be a good area to look for a small estate when I returned to England."

Ravina nodded and sipped her coffee.

"And with that in mind, Lady Ravina, I have managed to cross the infamous Stanton Grange from my list today. As you rightly said, the place is far too damp and dark for my liking.

"So would you care to accompany me tomorrow on a little trip. I plan to visit Charlford to inspect a house I have high hopes will prove suitable to purchase."

Ravina looked up, startled.

"Oh, well, I should spend some time here, checking on the horses and the tenants."

"Surely you can spare one more day from your busy schedule?"

Sir Richard's dark eyes gleamed in the firelight and Ravina had the odd feeling that he was laughing at her.

"I would appreciate your opinion, especially as I plan

to breed horses there and I am sure you have a great knowledge of what suits animals in these Southern counties."

Ravina hesitated.

"Of course, if Sir Michael has a prior claim on your presence and if you are already promised to visit the Priory once more, then – "

"No, certainly not!" Ravina interrupted crossly. "My time is my own. I would be delighted to accompany you. Do you intend to ride?"

"If we go over the hills, it will prove a fairly short journey and will be a useful workout for my horse. Then, the day after, if you would not mind my staying an extra day, I will take my leave of you and Miss Allen. I know your cousin will be pleased to bring the house back to its normal routine."

Ravina muttered some polite platitudes, her feelings a whirl of confusion.

Within a few minutes, she made her excuses and retired.

She spent a restless night, trying to work out why Sir Richard intrigued and annoyed her so much.

She finally decided it was because he had a knack of getting under her skin, of making her feel like a naughty child one moment and then his equal the next.

She knew, for example, that because he had constantly lectured her about riding alone, she would not tell him about Bobby Watson's warning.

Sir Richard did not know the Watson family and so might well think there was some substance in the boy's words, not realising that it was just a story to frighten a member of the Ashley family.

*

By the time the sun had risen above the trees in the orchard, Ravina had washed and dressed in her favourite blue riding habit.

She brushed aside Gibbs's anxious offer of breakfast and stopping only to take an apple from a bowl, she headed for the stables.

Sweetie was being groomed and whickered in delight at the sight of Ravina, knowing she would have sugar lumps in her pocket.

She had inherited her love of horses from her father and knew that for all her enjoyment of the hectic life in London, the parties and fetes, fun and gaiety, she was never happier than in the country among her ponies and horses.

As she turned to go back to the yard, she realised a buckle was loose on her boot and bent to fix it.

Suddenly she realised that there were two grooms in the stall next to her, dealing with Sir Richard's horse.

"Eee, Jacob, this is a fine animal."

"You're right there, Tom. Best stallion I've seen for many a year."

"How's his old leg, then?"

There came the distinct noise of Jacob's wheezing laugh.

"Naught wrong with his leg. Never was. Little scratch on the hock, that's all it was. I did be telling Sir Richard that, but he just said, 'yes, yes, let's keep him quiet for a couple of days.' None so odd as the aristocracy!"

"Ah, you're right there, Jacob. But we'd better get this beast saddled up. Sir Richard'll be here soon."

Ravina moved silently down the central passageway out into the cobbled courtyard where all was bustle and noise.

Sweetie was ready for her and she mounted, hardly

capable of thanking her groom, her mind was in such a spin.

Sir Richard strode into the yard just as Jacob walked his horse out into the sunlight.

Within seconds he had swung into the saddle and with a brief "good morning" to Ravina, he turned the horse's head and trotted out of the yard.

Automatically, she urged Sweetie forward and followed him.

She still could not believe what she had overheard. There had been nothing wrong with the grey stallion! It was all lies.

But why? What purpose had been achieved by his staying at Curbishley Hall for a few days?

She remembered the way she had met him at the ball in London and the very odd encounter at the hotel on the way to Dorset.

Was he following her?

A cold chill ran across her body. Could it be that he was *not* the English gentleman he said he was?

She knew her father kept all sorts of secrets and private papers in his study. Had this Sir Richard wanted access to the house to spy, explore, discover?

She stared at his broad back as they trotted swiftly down the drive and turned onto a path that led into the hills.

A spy? No, she could never believe that. Whatever this man was, he was surely honest. There must be some other explanation.

Then she recalled Bobby's words. She had been alone in the woods with Sir Richard.

Was that the danger Bobby had meant?

The track up the steep hillside was too narrow to ride two abreast. Sir Richard rode on first, occasionally shouting back comments about the state of the path, holding back a bramble with his whip, or advising on a different direction for her to follow as Sweetie's hooves slipped on the chalky ground.

They crested the ridge and reined to a halt, gazing down at the sweeping slopes that ran green and gold towards the sea, which was a kaleidoscope of blue and green and turquoise as the wind skimmed the surface.

Ravina felt the salt wind bringing colour into her face and laughed with the sheer delight of being out on such a glorious day.

A lark was singing unseen high in the sky above them and Sweetie bent her head to crop the turf studded with tiny blue and yellow flowers.

Sir Richard turned in his saddle and smiled at Ravina.

He thought he had never seen anything as beautiful as she looked at that moment. Her gold curls in tangles, her eyes bright and shining, a smattering of freckles across her nose.

"What a wonderful place England is on a day such as today," she exulted. "How beautiful the sea appears from up here. So smooth and peaceful. I love Curbishley Hall with all my heart, but sometimes I wish Papa had a home right on the beach."

Sir Richard stood in his stirrups and pointed with his riding crop to where a fold in the hills sheltered a honey-stoned mansion whose gardens ran down to the cliff top.

"That is our destination, Lady Ravina. Mitcham Manor. It stands empty as its owner recently emigrated to the New World where he has large estates – in Carolina, I believe."

"You are thinking of purchasing it?" Ravina asked as they walked the horses towards the house.

"Indeed so. As you can see, it has very fine stabling

and ample pasture for the animals I intend to breed. And that long stretch of sandy beach where I will be able to exercise them every day."

Ravina fell silent. Surely a spy would not be planning on buying a home such as this and planning a life when he would need to be on hand all the time to oversee such an ambitious undertaking?

"Can we see inside the Manor?" she asked as they trotted through a wide entrance between two stone pillars and along the soft turf by the drive.

Sir Richard nodded.

"Yes, indeed. I understand the rooms are large and airy with magnificent views of the sea from all the upstairs apartments. And I would be glad of your opinion. Obviously it is not as old as the Priory, but perhaps you will find some parts of it agreeable."

Ravina cast him a surprised glance. For a second, Sir Richard's voice had sounded almost sarcastic.

She supposed he was about to lecture her again on the suitability of her friendship with Sir Michael. Well, she would *not* listen. She would choose her own friends, as she had always done.

They had arrived at the bottom of the fine double stone stairway that led to the front door.

Ravina began to dismount, only to find Sir Richard was on hand to help.

For a second she was all too aware of how close they were standing, his grip on her arms, the way his shirt clung to his body under his jacket.

She knew if she raised her eyes, she would find that her face was only inches from his and she felt her heart give a slight quiver at the thought.

She could feel his breath warm on her cheek before

they parted as her riding boots touched the ground.

Sir Richard did not speak, but produced a large key and swung open the front door.

Ravina followed him into a hallway that was beautifully proportioned, with a double staircase mirroring the steps outside, rising in graceful curves to the balcony above.

Ravina exclaimed with delight as they moved from room to room, her admiration growing with every minute.

The manor house was indeed lovely. A warm welcoming home with rooms that were big enough to entertain in, but not so large that a family might feel lost in their vastness.

Upstairs was a selection of bedrooms, all individual in size and shape, good servants' quarters and a marvellous nursery wing with an old piebald rocking horse still in proud possession of the schoolroom.

"How sad. They have quite forgotten to take Dobbin with them," Ravina cried, smoothing back the wiry hair from his wooden painted head.

"I expect the children grew up and decided he was too big to ship out to America," Sir Richard commented.

"So, Lady Ravina, do you like the Manor? Do you think that with a little decoration and suitable furniture it would make me a comfortable home?"

Ravina walked across to the barred nursery window and stared out across the gardens and orchards to where she could just see the edge of the cliff that protected the house from the sea.

"Indeed, Sir Richard, I think the Manor would make a lovely home, but even with servants, you might find it a little large living here on your own."

He placed his hand on the rocking horse and gave it a

gentle push, watching the curved runners making little marks on the dusty floor.

"I am hoping that I will not be alone. There is a lady whom I would like to ask to be my wife and then – "

"Ouch!" Ravina winced. She had clutched the iron bars at the window so hard that a little sliver of metal had sliced into her finger.

Sir Richard intended to marry! This house was being prepared for his wife.

She felt a surge of anger and despair. He had no right to bring her here, to ask her opinion of its suitability. That was the prerogative of the lady to whom he would be offering his hand and his heart.

She had no idea why she should feel so upset. After all, this man was a stranger, he meant nothing to her!

Nothing at all.

"You are hurt, Lady Ravina?" Sir Richard enquired, moving to take her hand to inspect the blood that was swelling into a ruby drop on her pale flesh.

Ravina snatched her hand away.

"It is nothing, I assure you. Goodness, it is getting late. I must go home at once. Dulcie will be wondering where I am. And I have to make plans to visit the Priory tomorrow."

Sir Richard's face darkened.

"The Priory?"

"Indeed," Ravina replied brightly, clutching her handkerchief against the cut and trying to control the quaver in her voice.

"And if you live here in the Manor, Sir Richard, we may well be neighbours because I have every reason to believe that Sir Michael will shortly ask me to be his wife and I intend to say *yes*!"

CHAPTER EIGHT

When she looked back in the days that followed, Ravina could remember very little about her dreadful journey home from Mitcham Manor.

She had left the nursery, rushed downstairs, mounted her horse and with a silent and grim-faced Sir Richard trotting behind her, had ridden quickly back to Curbishley Hall along the roads, forgoing the hillside tracks.

So he was to marry – and soon. Mitcham Manor was to be this unknown woman's home.

Well, she wished the lady joy. To live with a man with so little sensitivity would be a great hardship.

Sweetie skittered as Ravina's fingers tugged on her reins as she forced her anguish to the back of her mind.

She was determined not to give Sir Richard the opportunity of thinking that his actions were of any concern to her.

"Are your plans now determined, sir?" she asked as they reached Rosbourne and trotted through the village.

"Yes. I fear I must impose on your hospitality for just one more night before I head for Dorchester. I have business there that will no longer wait."

Ravina paid lip service to the formalities, wondering bitterly if that was where the lady lived who one day would be his wife.

The woman who would be Mistress of Mitcham Manor, watch her children grow up in the nursery, run through the orchards and paddocks, gallop their ponies on the beach and –

With a great effort of will, she stopped the painful progression of her thoughts and thankfully saw the gates of Curbishley Hall appear.

Then, at last, they were safely inside the stable yard and she was kicking her feet free of the stirrups. But before one of the grooms could help her, Sir Richard was at her side.

Ravina slid from the saddle and for a brief moment felt the strength of the arms holding her. But even as she murmured her thanks, she refused to glance up into those dark penetrating eyes.

"Lady Ravina – " his voice sounded strangely unsure.

She could have even imagined that there was a touch of bewilderment in his tone.

But no matter. The last thing she wanted was for Sir Richard to guess her attachment towards him.

How embarrassing that would be.

She had no wish to see a sudden gleam of understanding in his eyes, no wish to see any sign of pity cross his face.

That would be unbearable!

Ravina hugged her anger and despair to herself, as she bade him a curt farewell and fled upstairs to the sanctuary of her room.

Here she threw herself full-length on her bed and beat at the pillows with clenched fists.

'How dare he take me to look at that beautiful house when all along he has been planning on bringing his bride there,' she screamed at herself.

Tears trickled down her face as her anger gave way to grief.

But why was she so upset? Sir Richard had never given her any inclination that his feelings towards her were anything but those of a censorious stranger.

Had she fallen in love without even realising it was happening?

Was it possible?

This turmoil, this upheaval.

Was this love?

'And I am so pleased I told him I am to marry Sir Michael!' she thought. 'He will never know that my affections had turned in his direction.'

But she knew in her heart of hearts that she was not pleased at all.

Ravina stayed in her room until dinnertime that evening. She told a concerned Dulcie that she had caught a little too much sun and had a slight headache but that it would soon pass.

Her cousin pulled the curtains across the window and produced a little pillow stuffed with camomile.

"Rest on this for a while," she fussed. "Really, Ravina, what would your dear Mama say? Riding without a hat in this weather! She would not be happy that I let you leave the house like that."

Ravina turned her head to one side, glad that the gloom in the room hid her tear-streaked face from view.

"Yes, I am sorry, I have been very stupid," she said softly. "But I will learn my lesson well, Dulcie dear."

Dulcie sat on the edge of the bed and stroked the wild gold curls back from Ravina's temple.

"Will you dine downstairs or shall I arrange for a tray to be served here in your room?"

Ravina hesitated.

She had no wish to face Sir Richard, but she was no coward. She refused to run away from him. This was *her* home and she would not skulk in her room like some naughty schoolgirl.

"Yes, indeed, I will be at dinner as usual, Dulcie. I am feeling better already. Perhaps you can ask cook for some asparagus soup, fish and a plain soufflé. I do not feel I can face a heavy meal."

"Certainly. By the way, we will be dining alone tonight. Sir Richard has told me that he will not be with us as he has to meet a friend in Lyme and will be dining out."

"I see."

Ravina slid off the bed as Charity came into the room.

The lady's maid helped her out of her riding clothes and boots and as Ravina sat at her dressing table, she found the tension in her shoulders easing as Charity began to brush her long blonde hair into a silky gleaming swathe.

So, that was that.

This unhappy episode in her life was now over.

Ravina would not see Sir Richard Crawford again, unless she was unlucky and happened to be present when he came to call on her parents to introduce his new wife.

"I thought Sir Richard was leaving us today. I fear we are in danger of becoming a hotel, Dulcie dear. Surely he must have other friends who would happily give him shelter while he looks for his new home."

Dulcie gave her cousin a concerned look. In all the time she had known Ravina, she had never heard her sound like this before. Perhaps the sun had really made her ill.

"Tomorrow I must ride out and visit the tenants," Ravina said brightly, leaning forward away from Charity's ministrations to pinch her cheeks until they glowed pink against her pale face.

"Papa will be annoyed if I do not show a regular interest. He always checks most punctiliously to take note of any problems they may be having."

She could see Dulcie standing behind her, reflected in the mirror. Her cousin was frowning.

"But Ravina, do you not already have a prior luncheon appointment with Sir Michael at the Priory?"

Ravina looked blankly back at her for a few moments and then recalled that she had, indeed, promised to return to the Priory to talk about Sir Michael's house-warming plans.

"Oh, yes, I had quite forgotten," she admitted drearily.

Dulcie turned away to pick up and fold a few garments that Ravina had left scattered across her bed.

How could Ravina forget Sir Michael? She was ashamed of her cousin. Sir Michael was such a kind and understanding man.

Her heart gave a little flip as she recalled the day she had spent with him discussing curtains. They had walked in the grounds of the Priory and she had admired the tidy layout of his gardens.

They had sat in a little gazebo away from the house and a footman had brought chilled lemonade and little macaroons.

For an hour they had talked and laughed and discussed the renovations. She had forgotten her lowly position in life, forgotten that she had no right to this man's attentions.

But only too soon it had been time to return to her duties.

Dulcie's hand went once more to the pocket of her apron and tightened round the crisp linen square that had belonged to Sir Michael.

It was all she had to remind herself of that day. All

she would ever have.

And as she left Ravina's room and walked downstairs to oversee the dinner arrangements, she wondered unhappily how she would cope if Ravina married Sir Michael and became Mistress of the Priory.

*

Upstairs, Ravina finally dismissed Charity and walked to the window, gazing out at the familiar woods and fields, the hills that led towards the sea and Charlford –

Dinner passed quietly. Ravina had no appetite but made an effort to eat her meal. She did not want Dulcie to start asking more detailed questions about her well-being.

But for some reason, Dulcie seemed distracted as well this evening. Neither had much to say and the conversation limped along.

"How did you know I was to visit the Priory again?" Ravina finally asked her cousin, trying to bring her mind back to everyday life, away from the dreams she was exploring so helplessly.

Dulcie's face went a bright shade of pink and she dropped her fork.

"Oh, Sir Michael called in for a moment this afternoon when he was passing. He mentioned your appointment and indeed, I agreed to go over to the Priory myself in the afternoon to help his housekeeper with a minor problem that has developed in the new servants' quarters."

"I am sure you will be extremely useful," Ravina said in a distracted fashion.

How could she possibly talk about furnishings and servants' quarters when her heart was breaking?

Because that was how she felt and she was both anguished and angry with herself.

She had to admit that Sir Richard had never given her

103

any sort of encouragement.

So why did she feel so bereft when she had never gained his affections in the first place?

No, she lifted her chin and blinked back the tears that were threatening to fall.

She was Lady Ravina Ashley and she would be as brave as all the other Ashley women had been in the past.

She would indeed visit the Priory tomorrow for luncheon and, whatever she had said earlier to Sir Richard, she would make it clear to Sir Michael that she was not interested in furthering their relationship.

Then the day after, she would set about returning her life to some semblance of normality.

Ravina vowed that once he had left Curbishley Hall for good, she would never think of Sir Richard Crawford and his deep brown eyes again!

She retired to her room as soon as it was polite to do so.

She was determined not to be up and around when Sir Richard arrived.

She lay in bed, unable to sleep at first, listening to the faint sounds of the clocks in the house striking the hours, wondering about the past few days and wishing her parents were home.

She desperately wanted to hear what her father had to say about Sir Richard, to discover if there was some secret he was keeping from her.

If she could hear something to his disadvantage, perhaps her liking of him would fade a little.

'Oh, I do wish Mama were here. I need to talk to her so badly. She is so wise. She would know how to make me feel better.'

Downstairs in the great hall, lamps had been left lit for

Sir Richard's arrival. A sleepy footman sat in the hall, trying to stay awake, waiting to see if he could be of any assistance.

Dulcie was making her final rounds, checking that the lower windows had been latched tightly and that guards had been placed in front of the fires.

She was about to retire to her room when the door bell rang and Stephen, the young footman, hurried to open the door for Sir Richard.

Dulcie turned and walked back down the stairs.

"Good evening, Sir Richard. Goodness, you look tired. Can I arrange for some food and drink for you?"

Sir Richard slapped his riding gloves across his legs to remove the dust.

"No, thank you, Miss Allen. I have dined already. A glass of brandy would be most welcome, however."

"Stephen will be pleased to attend you. I am about to retire but hope to see you in the morning before you leave."

Sir Richard bowed.

"Indeed. And has Lady Ravina already retired?"

"Yes, Sir Richard."

He turned as he was about to enter the drawing room.

"Dreaming about her forthcoming marriage, no doubt."

Dulcie stared at him, bewildered.

"Marriage?"

"Lady Ravina told me today that she would be accepting the advances of Sir Michael Moore."

Dulcie felt the world spin round and round and was grateful that she was holding onto the banister otherwise she knew she would fall into a faint.

"They are to marry? I-I – had no idea. Ravina has said nothing. *Married*? Well, you must excuse me, Sir Richard.

I am feeling a little tired and will leave you to your brandy."

Aware of his penetrating glance that seemed to see so much, Dulcie stumbled her way upstairs to her room, thankful to be able to shut the door so that no one could see the tears that were now trickling down her face, washing away all the silly lingering dreams about Sir Michael that she had clung to for the past weeks.

*

Even though she was sure she would not, Ravina must have slept before dawn, because the sky was quite bright when she opened her eyes.

She rang for Charity and gave orders for her breakfast to be served in her room. The hot tea and delicious fresh bread, newly churned butter and honey straight from the comb helped her feel better.

Ravina bathed and dressed with renewed energy. She would cope with whatever life threw at her and not be discouraged.

These feelings that had surfaced inside her for Sir Richard were surely only passing fancies, nothing more.

It was because she was alone or perhaps – and this was a sobering thought – because she had been flattered by the attention she received from men such as Giles de Lacy, Robert Dunster and Sir Michael, that she had expected every man she met to feel the same for her.

Well, she had discovered the error of her ways.

Sir Richard would soon be a married man and she had no time at all for girls who cast their hats at men who were already engaged.

The house lay still and quiet when she ran downstairs. Somewhere nearby one of the footmen was whistling and she could hear the housemaids cleaning the grates and the parlour maid laying the table for breakfast.

She had snatched up a hat as she left her bedroom. She knew Dulcie would be distressed if she rode out again bareheaded in the hot sunshine.

Ravina glanced at the clock in the hall as she passed. It was still very early but she was determined to be out of the house before Sir Richard and her cousin appeared.

'Admittedly I dare not arrive at the Priory too early for luncheon. That would be the height of bad manners, but I can ride through the woods for a while and calm my mind.'

A groom swiftly saddled Sweetie and she was just turning out of the stable yard when someone stepped out of the shadows and grasped the horse's bridle, bringing her to a halt.

It was Sir Richard!

"Lady Ravina – riding out early again?"

Ravina pulled the bridle out of his hands, but could not urge Sweetie forward with him standing in her path.

"Why yes, Sir Richard. I am on my way to visit my fiancé. We are planning a party to announce our engagement, so I would beg you not to delay me."

Sir Richard scowled darkly.

"Allow me to accompany you – or – " he went on ruthlessly, seeing the refusal on her face – "take a groom with you. There have been reports of a band of ruffians abroad in the countryside near here."

Ravina tossed her head.

"What nonsense is this? You have been listening to alehouse gossip by the sound of it, Sir Richard. I would have been told of any danger in this area. The staff here is always extra vigilant for my safety when my parents are away on one of their European trips."

"I must still insist – "

"Insist, sir?" Ravina's temper was beginning to fray.

How dare he accost her and act in this fashion, as if she was just a silly child.

"Well, I insist that you stand out of my way and let me be. Keep your advice for *your* fiancée!"

She tightened the reins, turned Sweetie's head and urged her on, ignoring Sir Richard's shout as the horse leapt forward, almost sending him flying into the mud of the stable yard.

Ravina galloped across the fields, leapt a hedge at the far side and did not stop until she was deep inside the woods.

She was so angry. That wretched man!

She had never met anyone before who could annoy her so much. The unknown woman who was to become his wife was welcome to him!

Eventually, after her headstrong flight, she realised that Sweetie was tiring and eased her down into a walk.

Suddenly Ravina remembered a little stream that ran through the woods. She turned the weary mare and pushed through the bushes and undergrowth.

Yes, there was the little clearing she recalled with a sparkling trickle of water running down a stony bed over a little waterfall.

She slid out of the saddle, led Sweetie up to the water and let her drink a little, remembering that she must not have too much while she was hot.

Then she tethered her loosely to a branch and sat down on a big flat stone to calm herself and gather her wits before confronting Sir Michael.

She realised that if she arrived looking hot and bothered, the gossips would start talking and her reputation would suffer.

She shut her eyes and allowed memories of all her meetings with Sir Richard to flood her mind.

They had fought and argued, but each time she had been in his company, she had felt more alive and happier than she had ever believed possible.

Could it be – *was this love*?

If it was, it was nothing to how she had once imagined it would feel.

She had liked other men before, enjoyed their company, flirted, danced and even considered one or two as possible husbands.

Ravina had always declared she would only marry for love. She had read of falling in love in so many romantic novels. She had thought it would be exciting, that she would feel butterflies in her stomach and that her heart would turn over every time she saw her loved one.

"You are supposed to lose your appetite, to feel faint when you see your intended," she murmured to a disinterested Sweetie.

So what was this deep, tearing sensation inside her? Was this love, the way her stomach clenched whenever she saw Sir Richard's tall dark figure?

The fizzing sensation she felt in her blood when she heard his voice?

Were all these symptoms of love? They were not mentioned in any of the many romances she had read or the ballads she had listened to all her life.

Ravina sighed.

Perhaps she was suffering from the onset of some illness? A bad chill could give you odd feelings.

She determined to consult Nanny Johnson when she returned home this afternoon. Surely her old nurse could give her a tonic that would help to disperse these sensations.

She sighed and raised her face to feel the sun as it

gleamed through the branches.

She closed her eyes.

'I will rest here for two more minutes,' she decided, 'then I will make my way to the Priory and see if I can make it clear to Sir Michael that I am not the woman for him.'

She felt the first smile of the morning cross her lips.

Indeed, there was a perfect match for him already living at Curbishley Hall!

She was convinced that warm feelings existed on both sides, but Sir Michael was being very male and silly about Dulcie's position in Society.

She frowned as a shadow fell across her face – the sun going behind a cloud – she opened her eyes and screamed.

A man – Heavens, it was *Joe Watson*, Bobby's father, standing right in front of her and even as Ravina started to jump to her feet, another man came up behind her and pulled her arms behind her back.

She twisted round sharply and came face to face with the industrialist, *Robert Dunster*!

"Mr. Dunster! Joe Watson. What are you doing – let me go at once! How dare you!"

Ravina struggled violently and managed to tug herself free, but she had only taken a step away when Robert Dunster caught her again.

She opened her mouth to scream, but his fleshy hand slapped against her mouth and she winced as he twisted her arm behind her back and began to propel her forward deep into the woods.

She kicked out and heard Robert Dunster swear in a vile manner as her riding boot caught him on the knee, but he was too strong for her.

Then Joe Watson was stepping up, an evil grin on his face, his big dirty hands tying a foul-tasting rag around her mouth.

She was dragged between them, her feet scuffing in the earth until they reached a narrow road when she was suddenly picked up and half thrown, half pushed inside a closed carriage.

She heard shouts and guessed that Joe had clambered up into the driving seat. Next came the crack of a whip, the jingle of bridles and the vehicle lurched forward.

As the carriage careered through the woods, fear coursed through Ravina, but she still struggled to stand up, to fight back against her cruel kidnappers, until with a curse, a ruthless hand pushed her down onto the floor.

She lay still for a while, trying to listen and work out where they were going. But the carriage twisted and turned, heading along a path through the woods.

She heard the rumble of the wheels as they crossed a wooden bridge and then they were on a road and travelling faster than ever.

Ravina gave up struggling. She realised there was no point. She must conserve her strength for when she was out of the carriage. Surely there would then be a chance to escape.

Her brain was spinning.

Had Robert Dunster gone mad? But he was not working alone. How could he have persuaded Joe Watson to help him in this mad dangerous escapade?

Well, Joe had no love for the Ashley family – that was true. He had never forgiven her father for dismissing Beatrice from her post as nursery maid.

'Oh, poor Bobby! To have such a man as your father,' Ravina thought. 'So his warnings to me about riding in the woods were right. But surely he isn't involved, too. Oh, now, please God do not let young Bobby be part of this foul plot.'

Suddenly the carriage swung violently round a corner and she was thrown against the side.

She tried to scream, but the rag in her mouth was tied too tightly and she could only make a moaning noise.

Robert Dunster lost his footing and fell between the seats and in the confusion Ravina managed to scramble upright.

She pushed her head through the open window in an effort to see where they were. But they were travelling too fast. All she could see was a blur of trees and bushes as they thundered past.

The wind tore her hair free from its pins and in desperation she tugged off the remaining blue velvet ribbon and flung it away, just as Robert Dunster regained his footing.

Still struggling, she was pulled back inside the coach and thrown against the side panels, banging her head.

For a second Ravina saw bright orange lights, then all was dark –

CHAPTER NINE

The next thing Ravina knew was that it seemed as though Charity had forgotten to pull the curtains and someone, somewhere was moaning quietly.

The room was too dark, Ravina's head ached dreadfully and she did not understand why her normal lace pillow had become rough and scratchy and had a dreadful smell.

She tried to sit up and groaned at the pain that lanced through her skull.

She touched her head just under the hairline and winced as her fingers came away covered in sticky blood.

It was all coming back to her now.

Robert Dunster had kidnapped her! She still could not believe it. What did he intend to do with her?

'Oh, dear God, help me,' Ravina prayed. 'He must have gone mad. This is not the behaviour of a sane person. I must escape from him.'

She swung her legs off the rough bed and gazed at her prison.

She was in a dark dingy attic. There were wooden shutters at the window and she could see sunlight glinting round the edge of the frames, but when she tried to open them, she realised that they had been nailed shut.

She stared around in desperation, then stumbled to the door and rattled the handle hard. But, as she had already suspected, it was locked fast.

The little room contained nothing that would be useful as a weapon. There was just the truckle bed and a dusty rug on the floor. Not even a chair she could use to hit whoever came through the door.

Ravina sat on the bed, her fists tightly clenched, fighting the desire to scream and cry.

She was determined she would not show Robert Dunster how scared she was of him. She refused to give him that satisfaction.

And if he – well, if he wanted some sort of sexual favour, then she would sell her honour as expensively as she could.

Her thoughts flew back to home, to Dulcie. When would her cousin realise she was missing?

'Oh, if only I had taken Sir Richard's advice this morning,' she wailed. 'Why was I so silly, so full of pride? He suspected that something was wrong in the neighbourhood, but surely even he could not have imagined this dreadful crime.'

So what would happen now? Sir Michael was expecting her for luncheon, but when she failed to appear, he would think she had either forgotten or decided not to come.

Would he be concerned?

'I doubt it,' Ravina muttered. She had the feeling that he was so engrossed in his own affairs that he would not worry about a young female's flighty attitude to an appointment.

Dulcie, of course, thought she was at the Priory and she had told Ravina she was going there herself in the afternoon to speak to Sir Michael's housekeeper.

Surely then Ravina's disappearance would come to light?

But then what? They would hunt, raise a hue and cry, find Sweetie – if the little mare had not slipped her reins and wandered off.

Would they find traces of the carriage that had taken her out of the woods?

Well, they might, but once the carriage had reached the road, how would they follow it?

'Oh, God, give me strength to overcome this. Let me see my dear mother and father again.'

And Sir Richard. The thought flashed into her mind but it seemed wrong to add him to her prayers.

Sir Richard was soon to be married. He had no feelings for her and so she must have none for him.

She pulled her mind away from memories of his dark eyes gazing intently down into hers as a sound outside the door brought her to quivering attention.

As she watched, the handle turned and in came Robert Dunster, carrying a pistol and a small leather writing case tucked under his arm.

"Ah, Lady Ravina. You are awake at last. Good."

Ravina spoke out firmly and clearly, determined not to allow her voice to tremble.

"Mr. Dunster, I have no idea what wickedness you are planning, but I beg you to let me go before you travel any further down the evil path you are now treading."

The red-faced industrialist just sneered.

"Tsk, tsk, your pretty words mean nothing to me, young lady. You can save your breath. All I need from you is a letter to your father. Here – paper, ink, pen. You will write what I dictate."

Ravina stared at him, mystified.

"A letter to Papa? But he is travelling in the Balkans, as you know only too well. It would be weeks before a letter reached him."

Robert Dunster smiled but the expression was far from genial. It sent a tremor of fear down her spine.

"A fast courier will be there by the end of the week. Once I have his reply, I will arrange for you to be released."

"You cannot possibly keep me here for two whole weeks!"

Ravina tried not to let her voice shake. She refused to allow this repulsive man to see how frightened she was.

Robert Dunster shrugged.

"It is entirely up to you. The quicker you write the letter, the quicker you will be released. I need your father to sign a certain Treaty with some influential Turkish politicians. The letter will make it quite clear what will happen to you, his only child, if he refuses."

Ravina drew herself up to her full height.

She suddenly felt all the lingering chains of childhood fall away and knew in that moment she had become her own person.

"*I refuse to write any such letter.* I will not be party to anything that forces my dearest Papa into doing something against his honour and conscience."

The heavily jowelled industrialist glared at her.

"Then I will write it myself, madam. And you will still stay here until I receive my reply."

He waved the pistol at her and grated,

"Let us both hope and pray that your father sees sense and signs the papers."

"But how can you possibly hope to escape, even if he does? You will be hunted throughout Europe."

She shuddered as the thought struck her that perhaps

he had no intention of escaping. Perhaps he would kill her anyway and then there would be no witness to his crime.

He laughed as he opened the attic door.

"I intend to leave Europe and go to live in the Middle East where I shall buy a large estate," he snarled.

"I am to be paid a fortune for '*arranging*' for Lord Ashley to sign the political agreement. And the life a man of money and position can lead in that part of the world is infinitely superior to anything here, where the accident of your birth controls just how much influence you have."

He leered at her.

"Who knows, perhaps at the end of two weeks, we'll know each other much better, Lady Ravina! You may wish to accompany me to share my new life!"

He was still laughing as he slammed the door shut behind him.

Ravina sank down on the bed and buried her head in her hands. She could not believe what was happening to her.

She remembered only too clearly all Sir Richard's veiled comments about safety and security and the way he had always seemed to be around during the past few days.

Had he guessed that she was in danger? Had he known that Robert Dunster was the evil genius behind the rumours he had mentioned?

Ravina questioned herself. Would she have listened to him if he had told her?

She felt the hot tears burn her eyes, knowing that her foolish pride would have rejected his words.

Look at how she had carelessly pushed aside Bobby Watson's warning yesterday. He had been so insistent that she did not ride alone through the woods. He must have had some idea of what was going to happen.

What a stupid, stupid girl she was.

Why had not she realised that Bobby would never have said those words to her unless he was truly concerned for her safety.

But no. She was so vain. She had trusted her own judgement of the situation, just as she had trusted her own judgement of Robert Dunster.

How faulty that had proved to be was now only too obvious.

And now – she stared bleakly – she was a prisoner facing a truly dreadful future and, what was worse, her dear Papa was going to be blackmailed with her life as the prize!

She shuddered and flinched as thunder suddenly rumbled overhead and she heard the hissing crack of lightning.

Clasping her hands together, she sent her thoughts spiralling outwards.

'Oh, Richard, if I am to die, I wish I had had the chance to tell you how sorry I am. And, oh, how I wish you were here to help me.'

*

At two o'clock that same hot afternoon, the fat placid pony that Dulcie always rode, ambled happily along the road leading towards the Priory.

It was, indeed, far happier than its rider. Dulcie's face was pale, her eyes still red-rimmed from the tears she had shed all night long.

She would have been content to stay at home in her room, but she had promised Sir Michael that she would speak to his housekeeper and she would not break her word.

'If I cannot make him happy as his wife, then I can at least make sure his house runs smoothly,' Dulcie thought drearily as she guided her pony round the final corner.

Then she looked up, startled, as a group of men

appeared out of the woods at the side of the road and stood watching silently as she rode past.

Dulcie kicked the pony into a faster trot.

The gang of scoundrels looked alarmingly villainous to her and she felt her heart pounding.

Suddenly, a thickset man wearing a dark coat appeared to gesture the other men back into the trees.

Dulcie felt the blood drain out of her face. It was a long time since she had seen that face, but she would never, never forget it.

The man in the black coat was the man who had cheated her father out of his money, caused his death and her downfall into poverty.

She had intended to enter the Priory through the kitchens. That way there would be no need to risk of seeing Ravina and Sir Michael together.

Dulcie knew that her courage was held together by very fine threads. The sight of her young cousin laughing and smiling, maybe even holding hands with the man she herself loved so deeply, would be more than she could bear.

But as a groom came running out to hold the pony's head, a familiar voice rang out and she flinched and staggered slightly.

Sir Michael's hands shot out to steady her.

"My dear Miss Allen! How enchanting to see you. But whatever is the matter? Are you unwell? You look extremely pale. Come inside. You must sit down immediately. Shall I send for a doctor?"

The concern in his voice brought tears to her eyes.

"Thank you, Sir Michael. I am – I am just a little faint, I fear. Perhaps I might trouble you for a drink of water?"

Sir Michael shouted to a servant to bring some immediately and a maid came running from the house with a glass.

He helped Dulcie out of the stable yard into the shady calm of the orchard.

She sank down on a wooden bench underneath an apple tree heavy with ripening fruit.

"You will have a fine crop of apples for your cider, Sir Michael," she remarked, trying to think of something to say that would divert his attention away from her. "I do hope your cook knows the right time to pick them."

Sir Michael's plain but kind face showed a flash of irritation.

"I could not care a single jot about cider, Miss Allen. I am worried about your health. You rode from Curbishley Hall in the midday sun on that slow pony. Why did you not take a carriage?"

Dulcie turned her face away, biting her lip. The answer to that question was, of course, that she was a servant to the Ashleys.

Oh, admittedly, she was a member of the family, but she was paid a salary as housekeeper and as such she would not abuse her position by riding in a carriage as if she was Ravina.

"Forgive me, Sir Michael. It was indeed stupid of me. I have, in fact, recently chided Lady Ravina for riding out in the hot sun. Now, I have taken up enough of your time. I must find your housekeeper and see if I can advise on her problems."

She stood up and turned to face him.

Sir Michael shook his head.

"My dear Miss Allen, I refuse to believe that a distress this deep is caused just by the sun. Please tell me, what has happened?"

Dulcie took a deep breath to steady herself.

"I have just seen a ghost from my past," she mumbled at last. "The man who ruined my father. He was in the woods, just the other side of the village."

Sir Michael frowned and reached out to grasp her hands.

"That is truly a terrible shock. But what on earth is he doing in Rosbourne? In the woods, you said?"

Dulcie nodded, trying to catch her breath which was skipping slightly at the touch of his hands on hers.

Sir Michael felt a wave of anger wash over him. He had no idea who this man was or what knavery he was up to, but if the rogue came within his grasp in the future, he would suffer for it.

Because he had realised he no longer cared that Dulcie had fallen out of Society circles. All he wanted to do was protect her from harm, make her life easy and comfortable.

Because *he loved her*.

He looked at her soft dark eyes, the brave tilt to her chin. He wanted to wipe away that worry line between her eyes and see her laugh.

She was not a young girl and she had none of the beauty or spirit of Ravina, but what she did have was a serene, peaceful character that soothed him.

Being with Ravina was like being in the same company as a beautiful, tiring whirlwind. Time spent with Dulcie was restful but invigorating.

Dulcie was a splendid woman and the one with whom he wanted to share the rest of his life.

And without thinking any more, he reached forward, tilted her face and bent to kiss her tenderly.

*

The afternoon sun was striking long shadows across the velvet lawns of Curbishley Hall, gilding the profuse roses in the gardens with gold lights.

Dark eyes blazing with frustration, Sir Richard Crawford paced up and down the front terrace, slapping his riding crop against the lavender bushes that stood in ornamental stone urns along the path.

But he was oblivious to the marvellous scent that hung in the air from the crushed flowers.

All his thoughts were turned towards Lady Ravina.

He knew he should leave Curbishley Hall – indeed, his horse was saddled and waiting for him.

But, he just wanted to see her one more time. He realised they had to part permanently – she was, after all, engaged to Sir Michael Moore, but her safety was his overwhelming concern.

If anything was to happen to that marvellous golden girl – !

Sir Richard glowered, his eyes brooding and unhappy. He pulled his gold half-hunter from his pocket – half past the hour of four!

Surely Lady Ravina and Dulcie would be home soon from the Priory.

Then he felt his pulses quicken.

An open-topped chaise had turned through the gates and was heading slowly up the drive towards him, a pony trotting behind it.

Sir Richard started to relax and then felt every nerve in his body quiver with apprehension.

Sir Michael Moore was seated in the chaise, but there was only one young lady sitting next to him on the red leather seats.

Dulcie.

Sir Richard stepped forward urgently as the carriage drew to a halt and Sir Michael jumped out to help Dulcie down and even in his turmoil, Sir Richard noticed how lovingly the older man's hands lingered on her arms.

"Sir Michael, Miss Allen, good afternoon to you both, but where is Lady Ravina?"

The couple turned, their faces twin pictures of surprise and bewilderment.

"Ravina? Why, I have not seen her at all today," Dulcie said.

"I believed that Lady Ravina was to favour me with a visit for luncheon," Sir Michael put in, "but she never arrived at the Priory. Indeed, when Miss Allen came over to see my housekeeper, we decided we had probably muddled up our invitations."

Dulcie hesitated.

Sir Richard could tell that she knew only too well that there had been no muddle and that Ravina had known she was due to have luncheon with Sir Michael.

"Perhaps she felt unwell and is in her room?" Dulcie suggested sensibly.

Sir Richard felt a cold shock course through him.

"No, I have already enquired of the staff. I wanted to make my farewells before leaving. Lady Ravina is not at Curbishley Hall nor in the grounds. And her mare is not in the stables."

Dulcie went pale and swayed. Sir Michael's arm shot out and tenderly he led her towards a stone bench overlooking the garden.

"But where can she be? Can she have had an accident? Fallen from Sweetie? But, oh, she is such a calm horse. She never bucks or shies."

"Perhaps she rode too far, dismounted for some reason and then the horse bolted," Sir Michael said, producing a large handkerchief as Dulcie was reduced to tears.

Sir Richard looked grave.

"Sir Michael, may I have a private word?" he asked.

Dulcie mopped her tears and stood up, pulling herself together with a bravery that appealed to both men.

"I must go inside. I will check with Charity and the other staff. They may know something and be scared of mentioning it to Sir Richard."

The two men watched her rush away and Sir Richard turned to his older companion.

"I must go to find her at once," he said briefly. "Sir Michael, what I am about to tell you is a great secret. Do I have your word that it goes no further than between us?"

Sir Michael looked alarmed.

"But of course."

"I am sometimes called upon by the Foreign Office to undertake small commissions for them. Recently I was asked by Lord Ashley to keep a watching brief on Lady Ravina in her parents' absence."

"What possible danger could Lady Ravina be in?"

"Through Lord Ashley, she is a target for certain groups of people, men with no honour or scruples, men who wish to influence her father in his judgements on the political scene."

Sir Michael stared at him.

"And you believe she has fallen foul of one of these men?"

Sir Richard nodded grimly.

"I do."

"Who would possibly harm a young girl for his own foul ends?"

Sir Richard hesitated for a long moment and then enquired,

"Do you know Robert Dunster?"

The older man looked at him in amazement.

"Dunster the industrialist? We have never met, but I know of him, of course. Why, you cannot possibly mean – ?"

Sir Richard slapped his riding crop against the palm of his hand, wishing it was Robert Dunster's head he was hitting.

"It is a strong suspicion, no more than that at present. But he has been seen in this district with a gang of men."

Sir Michael went pale.

"My God, Dulcie – Miss Allen – was upset earlier today because she saw the man who ruined her father lurking in the woods with a group of ruffians. Could that have been Robert Dunster?"

Sir Richard swore under his breath and nodded grimly.

"Very likely. So *he* was the man who cheated Mr. Allen out of his money. Why am I not surprised? And he was in the woods? God, then he has her already."

Sir Michael opened his mouth to comment, but realised that they were wasting valuable time.

"What can I do to help?" he asked simply.

"Good man. Collect a few of the largest and strongest of the staff here and follow me as soon as you can."

"But where are you – "

"Lady Ravina set off for your home this morning. I saw her go, across the fields and straight into the woods. I saw the direction she took. I will track her as far as I can. There must be some sign of her – somewhere."

Without another word, Sir Richard ran for his horse, but as he cantered across the fields and into the darkening woods, he knew that the chance of finding clues would become more and more difficult as the night fell.

He trotted through the woods. The path was not difficult to follow and he was sure that Ravina would have taken the most direct route to the Priory.

But after twenty minutes, he came out of the woods and as the slowly setting sun coloured the Western sky with every shade of rose pink and apricot, he stared down the slope towards the stable yard at the rear of The Priory.

He had reached the end of the trail and there had been no sign of the woman he loved!

"Damnation!" he swore under his breath, savagely turned the stallion's head and urged him back into the woods.

Where the hell had Ravina gone? There must be some sight of her or the mare.

Half way back towards Curbishley Hall, his horse suddenly threw up his head and neighed loudly.

Sir Richard swung round in the saddle as, from somewhere deep in the woods, an answering whinny sounded through the trees.

'That's Sweetie,' he muttered and urged the stallion off the track. They crashed down a slope until they reached a little stream.

Trotting swiftly through the water, they rounded a bend and there was Sweetie still tethered to a bush.

The little mare threw up her head and whickered happily to see them.

Sir Richard untethered her, let her drink at the stream and, his dark face grim with terror, gazed round at the signs of the struggle that had obviously taken place.

"If only you could talk," he said angrily to the horse. 'Yes, there is where the devil stood – behind this bush. And here, oh, God, here is where he dragged her into the bushes!'

Leading Sweetie behind him, Sir Richard urged his mount into the thick undergrowth.

Now the signs were even clearer. It was obvious Ravina had not gone quietly with her kidnapper.

But once the track reached the roadway, it was harder to follow the traces of her abduction.

The ruts made by the carriage were plain in the muddy areas, but as Sir Richard trotted along the darkening road, he realised that the marks from the wheels and the hooves were becoming fainter and fainter.

He felt his frustration growing. The sun had now set and a summer storm was brewing.

Heavy clouds were gathering swiftly overhead and in the distance came the ominous rumble of thunder and his stallion started and jittered across the road, his ears laid flat to his steel grey head.

Just as Sir Richard reached a sharp bend where the road split into three, the rain began to fall. Within seconds he was soaked as the wind gusted and flung the downpour against him.

He stared around him in desperation.

The carriage could have gone in any direction. There was no way he could tell. And any trace would soon be washed away.

'*Ravina*!' he groaned. 'My darling girl, what *is* happening to you?'

Then suddenly a glimmer of colour caught his eye.

He trotted across to the narrow road that turned sharply to the left.

There, fluttering on a bush was a length of bright blue velvet ribbon!

He knew exactly who it had belonged to. He had seen Ravina tying her hair back several times with a similar strip of material.

'Well done, you brave girl,' he sighed, picking up the

ribbon and wrapping it round his wrist. 'You've given me a
sign. Hold on, sweetheart, I am coming to rescue you!'

CHAPTER TEN

Ravina shivered violently as the attic room grew colder and colder.

The thin slivers of light that had shone in around the tiny window had long vanished. Night had fallen and with it had come the storm.

An oil lamp hung from the rafters and she was glad of the faint yellow beams it threw out.

She could hear heavy rain beating on the roof and knew there were trees close by because she could hear the wind whistling through the branches.

When Ravina pressed her ear against the shutters, there was the sound of running water – obviously a river or stream close by.

The oil lamp had been lit an hour earlier by a hard-faced woman who had carried in a small metal tray holding a pitcher of water, a bowl of roughly torn bread and a hunk of stale cheese.

Ravina had stared at her in amazement.

"Beatrice!" she whispered. "Beatrice Watson. It is you, isn't it?"

The woman was indeed her old nursery maid, but the thirteen years that had passed since she had been dismissed from service at Curbishley Hall had not dealt kindly with her.

Ravina remembered her as a handsome girl, hard-voiced, it was true, but always clean and neat. Nothing like the slatternly creature standing in front of her now.

"Aye, it's me, your Ladyship!" she replied sarcastically. "Beatrice Watson. Surprised you recognised me after all these years."

"But Beatrice, what on earth are you doing working for that evil man? I know your brother is involved, but he has always been in trouble with the law. You were an honest woman."

"What do you know about being honest?" Beatrice sneered. "Your father turned me out of Curbishley Hall with only a month's wages to show for all my trouble. I worked my fingers to the bone, lookin' after you – nasty little spoilt brat that you were. I was honest and look where that got me. Nowhere.

"You with all your money and fancy clothes. Well, you don't look too fancy now, do you?

Her eyes gleamed and she ran her hands through her black untidy hair tangled around her head.

Beatrice stepped towards Ravina and she was convinced that she had been drinking, she was so wild and out of control.

"Joe and me is goin' abroad to work for Mr. Dunster when he leaves England. He's goin' to have a great house and land and horses and riches you can only imagine. And I'm to be his housekeeper and Joe will run the estate. We'll be rich. Mr. Dunster will see to that."

Ravina stared at her in despair.

She could see from the gloating expression on the woman's face that there was no chance of persuading her that this was all a fairy story, made up by Robert Dunster to persuade these poor uneducated people to join him in his criminal activities.

Ravina stared at the open attic door, wondering if she

could push past her and make a break for freedom, but she could see that it would be useless because the dark shape of a man – she thought it must be Joe Watson, lurked outside in the gloom of the passageway.

"Please – listen to me, Beatrice. I do not know what Mr. Dunster has promised you to keep me here, but I swear my father will double the amount if you let me go. And he will not prosecute you or your brother, I swear."

Ravina stretched out her hand but Beatrice ignored it. She just laughed and then turned and walked out, slamming the door behind her and Ravina heard the key turn in the lock.

She sank back onto the hard bed, overwhelmed with despair. Her foot hit the tray.

'I will not eat his horrid food,' she muttered to herself, but stopped and considered. She felt so weak and tired. Food was essential.

So she gritted her teeth and choked down the stale offering. At least the water was cool and refreshing.

And she was proved right as she could feel a little strength beginning to return to her weary limbs.

'I must escape. I must get home and warn Papa to ignore any letter he receives from Robert Dunster.'

Once again she hunted round the room for a weapon, a tool, anything she could use to help her free herself.

She looked at the oil lamp, wondering if she could perhaps throw it against the door and burn her way out. But in her heart of hearts she knew it would not work.

She pulled at the window shutters, but a great rusty nail had been twisted around the catch and she could not move it.

'Oh, God, please help me. What can I do? No one will ever find me here.'

She turned away in desperation and her foot caught the metal tray she had left on the floor and sent it flying.

She jumped at the noise it made crashing against the wall and then she stared at it.

In seconds she was examining the flat thin metal.

The ends of the tray were narrow but hard. This was no cheap, imported tin, but a sturdy old farmhouse implement made of iron.

Ravina carried it across to the window and pushed the end of the tray under the nail head and using every ounce of her strength, she struggled to force the nail to move.

At first nothing happened and she felt hot tears of frustration gathering in her eyes.

But the stubbornness that her parents had always seen as one of her greatest faults came to her rescue.

She refused to give up.

She would not be beaten!

She braced her feet hard on the wooden floor and, ignoring the pain in her fingers where the sharp edge of the tray was biting into her skin, she heaved at the nail again and to her joy it began to move.

Agonisingly slowly, the rusty metal gave way and the nail snapped in half. Immediately the wooden shutters sprang apart and Ravina could see that they had covered a window which was easily opened onto the dark wet night.

She peered out, blinking as the rain beat against her face, but glorying in the feel of the wet night air.

'I am sure I can squeeze through the window space,' she schemed, as she lifted the lantern to see what lay outside.

The flickering light from the lamp reflected against the driving rain, but she could see a tiled roof about six feet below the window.

It was steeply pitched, covered in slime and moss.

She was sure it would be very slippery, almost impossible to walk on.

Beyond the cottage, Ravina could see a black mass, unbroken by any light. She was sure that she was looking at dense dark woods.

Just then lightning flashed and lit up the whole area. As she had guessed, a river ran past just twenty yards away.

Ravina stared at the tiny window space. Her riding habit was heavy and thick. Even if she managed to crawl outside, the rain would make it impossible to move quickly.

She hesitated, but not for long.

She pulled off her skirt and jacket and stood shivering in her petticoat and bodice.

'If Dulcie could see me now,' she thought wildly. 'She would faint and never recover!'

Just then a noise outside the door made her flinch. Someone was coming up the stairs, someone with a heavy masculine tread.

Robert Dunster!

Without thinking twice, she thrust herself through the window and began to wriggle free.

And just as she was about to jump down onto the tiles below, the attic door opened and Robert Dunster roared his anger at her escape –

*

A quarter of a mile away, Sir Richard was trotting through the night, his eyes searching through the dark for any sign of habitation.

He had been forced to pull his horse back from a canter as the light failed, but the stallion was sure-footed and with Sweetie on a leading rein behind them, they were still making progress.

'Oh, Ravina, *where are you*?' he murmured in anguish.

The rain was pouring down harder and harder and suddenly a crack of lightning pierced the sky and thunder rumbled overhead.

The sudden summer storm was growing in ferocity and the track was becoming muddier, the horses' hooves slipping and sliding.

Sir Richard could hear rushing water to his left. Obviously a river was filling rapidly and roaring over its stony bed.

'God, I only hope my darling girl has some shelter. Surely even Dunster would not expose her to these conditions.'

Just then, as he rounded a bend, there came another great flash of lightning and, directly in front of him, Sir Richard saw an incredible sight.

A small house built on the banks of the river was lit up as if it was daytime.

And there, lying on the sloping roof, a slim figure draped in thin white garments was Lady Ravina herself!

She was desperately inching away from a thickset man who was halfway through the window, reaching out his great fleshy hands to pull her back.

Flinging himself off his horse, Sir Richard raced forwards.

"Ravina! *Ravina.* Jump. Quickly, my darling. Jump and I will catch you. Trust me."

"Sir Richard!"

His heart leapt at the joy in her voice and she slithered faster down the slippery tiles.

"Trust me, sweetheart. I would never let you fall."

Suddenly there was a flash and a crack rang out.

Robert Dunster had produced a pistol and was shooting at them!

With a scream, Ravina flung herself off the roof and the next second Sir Richard was holding her slim wet body close to his.

He buried his face in the soft damp curls that tangled around her face and thanked God with all his might that she was safe.

"Sir Richard – Dunster – kidnapped me – Beatrice – Joe – letter – Papa – " she panted disjointedly.

He did not stop to ask or reply.

Swiftly he swung her up into his arms and raced for the cover of the woods as another shot rang out.

"The man's gone mad," he snapped as he tenderly put Ravina down and draped his riding cloak around her body.

She was shivering violently, but he noticed, proudly, her eyes were sparkling and there was no sign of fear on her face.

"He wanted me to write a letter to Papa forcing him to sign some special document."

Sir Richard nodded.

"I have been trying to keep you safe for days, my sweet! Your father gave me strict instructions because there were rumours that some such plot was afoot. But you have not been an easy person to guard."

He glanced over his shoulder at the wild waving branches. Were they safe here? He doubted it.

And where was Sir Michael with the reinforcements? Surely they could not be too far behind.

"He did not touch you – hurt you in any way, because, damn his eyes, I'll kill him if – ?"

Ravina reached up a hand and placed it softly over his mouth, smiling as he kissed her palm.

"Hush! No, he threatened, but apart from rough handling me through the woods and into the cottage, he did no more but try to terrify me."

She looked up, trying to see his face in the dark.

"But, Richard, there are two other people inside the cottage. Beatrice, my old nursery maid, and her brother, Joe Watson. They are villains, but I still would not have them harmed, because I truly do not believe they really knew what Robert Dunster was doing or why."

Sir Richard suddenly pulled her close to him once more.

"Ravina – " he said hoarsely, "I know this is not the time or place, but you have to know now, before anything else happens to us, that *I love and adore you* with all my heart. You are the bravest, dearest, most wilful girl I have ever known and if you do not marry me, you will condemn me to live on my own in that beautiful house by the sea."

Ravina felt every nerve in her body sing with joy.

He loved her! This dark, difficult, dear man loved her as much as she loved him.

She had never thought love would come to her like this. But as unexpected as it was, it was glorious.

"I thought you had already chosen a wife. That day when we explored Mitcham Manor, you said – "

"I meant *you*, you silly goose!"

"I love you so much too with all my heart," sighed Ravina.

And ignoring the rumbling thunder and the rain that beat down on them, he tilted her face up to his and kissed her, tenderly and slowly at first, and then with deepening passion.

When they parted, he smoothed the rain soaked hair away from her face.

"Why are you smiling? Am I so amusing?" he asked wryly.

Ravina tried to hold back a giggle.

"I was just thinking that whether you want to or not, you will have to marry me now because you have seen me in my bodice and petticoat!"

Sir Richard began to laugh, then yelled and threw Ravina to one side.

She crashed down into some bushes, wincing as they cut her skin.

Dazed and frightened, she realised that Robert Dunster had leapt out of the dark and he and Sir Richard were struggling and fighting, their curses filling the air as the thunder crashed overhead and lightning split the darkness, over and over again.

Dunster's powerful arms seemed to be crushing the younger man, but Sir Richard was forcing him backwards through the undergrowth.

Sobbing, Ravina followed them, the world a whirling chaos of wind and rain and swaying branches.

Suddenly she realised the noise she could hear above the wind and the rain was the roaring of the river and when a hissing crack of lightning flashed once more, she could clearly see the struggling couple.

She gasped in horror.

"*The river bank*! Be careful. Richard, watch out. The bank is crumbling!"

But even as she spoke, the soaken mud silently gave way and the two men plunged into the raging torrent.

Ravina screamed and threw herself forward flat into the mud.

"*Richard*! Richard."

Oh, God, surely she was not going to lose him now. Not when they had just found each other.

The surface of the raging water remained unbroken and then a dark head bobbed up and Sir Richard was swimming strongly towards her.

Spluttering he clambered up the bank and she reached out to help pull him out of the river.

Kneeling together, muddy and wet, they held each other close as the rain poured down and the river hurried Robert Dunster's body away to the sea.

And it was there, on the muddy river bank, locked in each other's arms that Sir Michael and his men found them.

*

On a bright autumn day, two families gathered to witness a very special wedding.

The week before in the ancient Church at Rosbourne in a quiet, sedate, old-fashioned but happy ceremony, Sir Michael Moore and Miss Dulcie Allen were married.

Lady Ravina Ashley and Sir Richard Crawford had been honoured guests and Ravina felt that she had never seen her cousin look so gloriously serene.

Safe in the knowledge that Sir Michael was following his heart and marrying the woman he truly loved, Dulcie had blossomed and the tense frown and down-turned mouth had been replaced by a glow of happiness as she contemplated her new life as Mistress of the Priory.

But the wedding that the whole County had been waiting for was to take place the following week.

Lord and Lady Ashley, home at last from their travels in the Balkans, had been surprised but pleased to discover that their daughter had given her heart and hand to Sir Richard.

The dastardly plot to destabilize a Government had been foiled and although Lord Ashley shuddered to think of the danger his daughter had been in, he knew that now the world was a safer place at least for a few years.

He laughed and sighed as he hugged her closely in a

138

rare show of emotion.

"I thought I told you to stay away from trouble, young lady?" he scolded, his voice tinged with the knowledge of what might have happened.

Ravina kissed his cheek.

"Dearest Papa! I wasn't even aware of the danger until it happened. But luckily there was Richard to keep me safe – just as you had planned."

*

Lady Ashley came to her room one evening and sat stroking her daughter's hair as they discussed everything that had happened.

"And you are completely sure of your feelings for Sir Richard?" her mother asked. "You have not in any way confused gratitude with love, my dear child? Because that is not the right basis for marriage."

Ravina smiled at her with a joy in her eyes that immediately dispelled her mother's doubts.

"No, Mama. I love him completely and utterly, more than I can possibly say. I would willingly follow him to the ends of the earth and back."

And Lady Ashley felt all her worries fade away, knowing that her daughter had found the one man who would be her soul mate for ever.

Beatrice and Joe Watson had vanished. Rumour had it that they had left the cottage under cover of the storm and fled to America.

Ravina could not help but feel relieved.

Although upset, poor Mrs. Watson would be better off without her abusive husband and Bobby was a youth who could make something of himself in service to Sir Michael.

Ravina would not have wanted to be responsible for prosecuting his father and aunt for kidnapping.

Nanny Johnson had cackled cheerfully to herself when Ravina had come running into her room to tell her the news of her engagement.

It had made the old nurse's heart glad to see the joy on her young lady's face. She had always known that it would take a very special man to win Ravina's hand and she was convinced that Sir Richard was just that person.

Nanny had known Lord Ashley since he was born and knew exactly how clever a man he was.

Had he chosen Sir Richard to be his daughter's secret guardian, hoping for this outcome?

Well, he would never say, but the old lady had her suspicions.

*

In the vast Cathedral, in front of a congregation of their friends, neighbours and notables from all aspects of Society, Sir Richard turned round at the altar as the organ played and watched, stunned, as a vision floated up the aisle towards him.

Escorted by her father, Ravina in white silk and lace with a long train and floating veil was a picture of loveliness.

She was holding a bouquet of pink roses and gleaming white lilies and only she and her husband-to-be knew that buried amongst the flowers were tiny blue and yellow blossoms from the slopes above their future home on the Dorset coast.

Sir Michael and Lady Moore were there to watch, linking hands and smiling at each other.

And in pride of place in the family pew sat Nanny Johnson, resplendent in a new outfit and wearing a magnificent hat decorated with two huge curled feathers that completely hid the view from the gentleman sitting behind her!

The familiar words rang out, rings were exchanged and Ravina pushed back the veil from her face to accept his tender kiss.

"I love you, my darling wife," Sir Richard murmured and Ravina trembled at the passion in his voice.

"With all my heart and soul for now, forever and till the end of time."

They were married!

This love she had found had been so very unexpected and delightful and her happiness knew no bounds.

But Ravina knew, as his grip tightened on her fingers and his lips touched hers in love and joy, that the future they would make together lay before them, as bright and shining as the sea they would lie and watch from their bedroom for so many years to come.